Billionaire Unveiled

THE BILLIONAIRE'S OBESSION
Marcus

J. S. SCOTT

Billionaire Unveiled

Cover by Wax Creative

ISBN: 978-1-946660-03-9 (Print)
ISBN: 978-1-939962-97-3 (E-Book)

Contents

Prologue

Dani

A Year Ago…

I knew I was going to die.

The only question was how long I had to live before the rebel group of terrorists who had kidnapped me would finally execute me.

I was hurting so badly that I was grateful when I lost consciousness. I had no idea how long I'd been imprisoned. It seemed like years, like I'd lived in this perpetual state of pain, deprivation, and humiliation for what seemed like forever. I'd tried to keep track of the days passing by, but I'd probably lost a few.

How long had I been like this?

A week?

Two?

Had I lost more days than I'd thought?

Death would pretty much be a blessing. I'm not sure how much more of their torture I can take. I'm not getting out of here. The

US wouldn't bargain with terrorists, and I'm never going to escape. Even if I had the opportunity, I don't have the strength to get away.

It's not that I wanted to die, but there was only so much agony a person could endure before they hoped for some reprieve, even if it meant they'd only find that relief from death.

At least it was late into the night, a small portion of the twenty-four-hour day that I'd come to welcome because the terrorists were all sleeping. It was the only time I wasn't terrified they'd decide to stroll in to torment me.

I was curled into a ball in the middle of the dirt floor, trying desperately not to think about food, water, or the fact that every inch of my body felt like I'd been used as a punching bag.

Reminding myself that my sacrifice had meant that some teenagers had been able to get their butts back across the border to safety was a fact I tried to hang onto with everything I had. I'd probably have to die so a bunch of kids could live.

It was a decent trade-off, right? If it was one or the other—which it had been—it was better for one person to die than a bunch of kids.

My issue with my reasoning was that I really didn't *want* to die. The survivor in me wanted *all* of us to live.

Unfortunately, the tiny portion that was left of my rational brain told me that wasn't possible.

I tried to take a deep breath, but it hurt so bad to breathe. I exhaled gently, trying to convince myself that for now, I was alone and wasn't likely to be disturbed until daylight.

No sooner had I told myself I was safe for a few hours, when a big hand slapped over my mouth with absolutely no warning. I fought the adversary, determined not to go down without a fight, even though I had very little strength.

I always fought.

It was just the way I was wired.

The nighttime was mine, the only chance I had to think—if I could stay conscious—and it pissed me off that the few hours I had to rest were being taken away from me.

I was sick of being a source of entertainment for the rebels whenever they wanted to torment me. I wished they'd just kill me and get it over with. If they did, the fighter in me would remain forever silent.

"Danica. It's Marcus Colter. I'm getting you out of here. Stay quiet."

The harsh whisper finally invaded my sluggish brain. *Marcus Colter?* What in the hell was he doing *here?*

I had to wonder if I was getting delusional. Marcus was an international businessman, a custom suit-wearing billionaire. Yes, he *did* always seem to show up in dangerous areas of the world. But why would he be in the desolate camp where I was being held prisoner?

I stopped trying to fight him, realizing that he was attempting to help me. "Marcus?" I said weakly once he'd uncovered my mouth.

He didn't speak, but he made a big slashing gesture for me to stop making any noise, and I could see it pretty plainly in my dimly lit prison.

Normally, I didn't like Marcus Colter. When we were in a civilized environment, we did nothing but antagonize each other. But right now, his voice gave me a glimmer of hope. At the moment, he was more friend than foe. Squinting into the darkness, I tried to make out the features of his face, but his form was pretty much a shadow, a man dressed entirely in black.

He met no resistance as he picked me up. I wrapped my arms around his neck with whatever strength I could muster, staying as quiet as possible as he carried me past the tents and out of the place where I'd thought I was going to breathe my last breath.

I buried my face in his neck, absorbing his scent like a sponge thirsts for water. He smelled like safety and freedom, and after all I'd been through at the hands of the rebels, it was an irresistible smell.

It seemed like he walked for hours until we arrived at a Jeep. Marcus jumped in quickly, holding me on his lap, the vehicle sprinting into motion the moment we were settled.

I couldn't speak. Not only was the action difficult due to my dry mouth and my cracked lips, but everything that was happening seemed…surreal.

Was I really being rescued or was I delirious?

My brain was so muddled that I just didn't know.

Getting my freedom back wasn't something I'd expected. I'd been resigned to the fact that I was *never* going to make it beyond the camp where I was being imprisoned.

The only thing I knew is that I *wanted* this to be real. But it didn't make sense.

And why was Marcus Colter here?

At one time, he'd done some private rescues of international prisoners, but his group had disbanded some time ago. My brother, Jett, had been injured in the ill-fated mission that had been the last for Marcus and the Private Rescue Organization. The only way my rescue could be happening is if he'd gotten the team back together again.

I suppose it wasn't impossible that he'd pulled a group of guys together. But my brother was definitely out of commission, and so were a few others who'd been wounded in the helicopter crash that had ended PRO's existence.

I wanted to thank him for risking his life to save mine, but I couldn't quite get the words out of my mouth. Maybe I'd always hated him for what he'd done to my older sister, Harper. But the incident with my sibling had occurred over a decade earlier, and I *was* grateful that Marcus Colter had snuck over the border and into Syria to rescue me. The mission was almost suicidal, yet he'd done it.

I moaned softly from the pain as the Jeep came to an abrupt stop and Marcus shifted my body to get out of the vehicle, and then handed me over to somebody in a helicopter.

I made it out. I'm going to live.

The realization that I wasn't going to die at the hands of my black-hearted tormentors was almost too much to comprehend.

Tears of relief trickled down my cheeks, but my body was so weak that I couldn't move. My mind was sluggish from deprivation and torture, but I knew everything I needed to know:

I was safe.

I felt much better a few days later as I ended my call with Harper to let her know I was still alive, and that I was getting more physically stable every day.

Maybe I *did* need to gain a few pounds, but with my love of all things junk food, I'd regain the weight I'd lost. I was well hydrated with the help of IV fluids, and my brain was finally functional again.

Dropping my cell phone onto the bedside table, I mumbled to myself, "I need to get the hell out of here."

There was nothing I hated more than hospitals, and I'd already been in the large medical facility in Istanbul much longer than I could tolerate.

Truth was, I wanted out of the Middle East. I wanted to be back on US soil.

"Talking to yourself again?" Marcus Colter drawled as he strolled through the door of my hospital room.

I wished I could deny his claim, but I'd been completely alone until he'd walked in, and it was obvious that I was done with my phone call. Honestly, I *did* tend to talk to myself a lot since I was usually alone. "I'm bored," I said. It was a lame excuse, but it was *partly* true.

I hadn't been out of my hospital bed except to use the restroom since I'd been admitted to the hospital. I wasn't used to being idle. My job as a foreign correspondent kept me traveling and extremely busy almost every minute of the day.

I looked up at Marcus as he stopped at my bedside, noting that he looked as handsome as ever in a custom suit and tie that almost matched the gray of his eyes.

"You'll survive," he drawled with very little sympathy. "You need to stay until your condition improves. You have to be strong enough to travel."

As usual, I wanted to slap the smug look off his face. Unfortunately, I'd seen the exact same expression too many times in the past. Everywhere I went, it seemed like Marcus was there. If a certain area of the world was a hot spot, I never had any question as to whether or not Marcus would show up. He always did, although I had no idea *why* he always seemed to be in the most screwed-up places in the world. Being a journalist, I had good reason for being wherever there was trouble. But Marcus was a businessman, and he no longer did any work with PRO. So why was it that he was always in the middle of anything bad that was happening on the planet?

"I'm better," I argued. "I'm strong enough."

Marcus lifted an arrogant brow. "You wouldn't make it past the hospital door before you collapsed," he observed. "You're still too weak."

I wanted to challenge him by getting up and walking out of the hospital, but I was still attached to the IV, and I already knew how much effort it took just to get up and go to the bathroom. I'd done it many times since they were pumping me full of fluids. I crossed my arms over my chest. "I want to go home, Marcus. If I have to, I'll have one of my brothers come get me."

I knew I was acting like an ungrateful brat, but the truth was, I was feeling really edgy and anxious. Fear was getting the best of me at the moment, and I couldn't stop the nightmares I'd been having, or the feeling that the rebels might somehow find me.

He shook his head. "They wouldn't do it. I've already talked to everybody in your family. Nobody is letting you out of the hospital until you're stable. It's a long damn trip back to the States. You need more time to get stronger."

I let out an irritated sigh because I knew he wasn't bluffing. Marcus wasn't the type to *not* back up every word he uttered. If he said he'd talked to my family, I *knew* it was true.

Honestly, I wasn't sure exactly *how* I felt about Marcus Colter now. My phone call with Harper had been intriguing. And it *had* let the eldest Colter brother off the hook for being an asshole to my sister, Harper. It was hard to believe it had been *Blake*, Marcus's identical twin, who had slept with my elder sister and broken her heart over a decade ago. That had been one of the reasons why seeing Marcus unsettled me, but it wasn't the only one.

Marcus could easily be the most stubborn, cynical, irritating ass I knew, and he hadn't changed a bit since the last time I'd seen him.

However, he *had* saved my life.

Before, I'd always had a reason to dislike him over what had happened with Harper. Now, I wasn't sure how to treat him. Yeah, he was still a jerk sometimes, but other than his overinflated male ego, I really had no reason to hate him anymore.

"So when can I go?" I asked in an annoyed tone. "I'll go stir-crazy if I stay here much longer."

"You just got hydrated. It's going to be at least another week."

I rolled my eyes. "It's just a plane ride to get back home."

Really, all I wanted was to get out of the Middle East and back to the US. I'd feel safer, but I didn't want to tell Marcus how nervous and tense I was feeling. Technically, I was in a safe place, and I didn't want to sound crazy or paranoid.

The two of us had always had a fairly level playing field. This area was my turf, the place where I did most of my reporting.

Now, it was the setting for most of my nightmares.

He dropped a large bag he'd been carrying onto the bed beside my hip. "Here's something to combat your boredom."

I rummaged through the sack, finding some books I'd wanted to read, a deck of cards, some of my favorite junk food, and a small chess set. "You play chess?" I asked. "Obviously I can't play alone."

He nodded. "I do."

"How did you know that I played?" I queried.

He shrugged. "Jett might have mentioned it."

I smiled. "None of my brothers can even challenge me anymore."

"I'll win. I always do," Marcus told me arrogantly.

I eyed him carefully as I opened a bag of chips and started munching on them like I'd been deprived. I let the salty taste flow over my taste buds, and I nearly moaned with satisfaction. He opened the small chess set and started setting up the pieces as I watched. Marcus radiated power, control, and a hefty dose of self-confidence, which was a nice way of saying he could be an arrogant prick. But that didn't mean I could ever forget the fact that his mere presence filled the room with tension.

I'd done little but trade jabs with Marcus in the past, and I wasn't sure quite how to interact with him now that I knew he wasn't responsible for sleeping with Harper and hurting her so badly.

"Chips?" I asked, offering him the open bag.

He frowned. "No, thanks. I avoid processed foods and excess salt. That stuff is bad for you."

I shrugged, pulling the chips back. I was only giving him one shot. I was greedy when it came to my snacks. "If I give up everything that isn't good for me, life would be boring."

After being deprived of food for so long, I planned on devouring every healthy and unhealthy bit of food I could get.

"Your brother, Jett, says the same damn thing," Marcus answered in a disgusted tone.

"I guess it's a family thing," I joked.

"I suppose."

"Do you think Harper and Blake will end up together now that the whole mess from ten years ago is finally settled?" I wanted my sister to be happy, and I was pretty sure Blake was the only man in the world who could make Harper settle down. In the decade since they'd parted, my sister had dedicated herself to her career as an architect, and I'd never seen her interested in another guy.

"I have no idea," Marcus answered as he took off his suit jacket and rolled up his sleeves. "I try not to get into other people's business, especially my family when it comes to their love lives."

I shifted position, sitting up in the bed so I could study the chessboard. "She loves him," I said confidently. "I'm not sure she ever stopped."

"I don't think Blake did either," Marcus admitted.

I nodded. "Then I'm sure they'll sort everything out."

"I hope so," he said in a graveled voice. "If they don't, he'll be moping around like an adolescent."

Deciding that I wanted the black pieces, I spun the board around. "I don't believe that you don't care whether or not your twin is happy."

"I didn't say that I didn't care," he reminded me.

So he does care, but he tries not to get involved? If I judged by Marcus's attitude on the surface, I'd be tempted to believe he really *didn't* give a crap about anybody but himself. But his actions told another story. He'd immediately found Blake once Harper had come to him about my kidnapping, and told his twin brother to straighten the mess out. He'd thrown the two of them together on purpose. I was sure he had.

"So you'd be happy if it happened?" I queried.

He didn't answer immediately. Marcus's gaze was on the chessboard since he got the first move with the white pieces, a position that gave him a slight advantage.

"Regardless of what you might think of me, I want my brother to be happy," he replied simply.

I soon found out that prying information out of Marcus was going to take more energy than I had. Unfortunately for me, the guy was an amazing chess player, and I was beyond sorry that I'd allowed him any advantage after he kicked my ass.

Thankfully, he wasn't the type to gloat too much, but it annoyed me just the same.

It took almost a week to the day I entered the hospital to get back out again. I still had some healing to do, but I was relieved when Marcus's jet finally got into the air to take us back to the US.

Tate Colter, Marcus's younger brother and the pilot of my rescue mission, had left yesterday morning, eager to get back to his wife, so

I no longer had the distraction of his company. I liked Tate, and I was just as grateful to him as I was to Marcus for risking his life to save me and keeping me company while I'd recovered. I hadn't gotten a chance to thank the rest of the team because I'd been too sick when they'd left, but I was truly thankful to all of them.

I leaned back against the leather headrest as Marcus's large jet climbed to its cruising altitude. "Thank you for coming to get me," I said in a breathless voice.

Never once had I mentioned my experience with my kidnappers. I answered questions, but I hadn't wanted to talk about it. I still didn't. But I'd thanked Tate before he'd left, and I knew I owed Marcus for taking such a major risk for somebody he barely knew.

"Just try to contain yourself from jumping back into another bad situation," he answered from the seat next to me. "I get why you did it, but you had to have known that you were probably going to end up dead when you crossed the border."

We hit turbulence while the jet was climbing, and I dug my short fingernails into the leather armrest. I'd never been a nervous flier before this trip home, but I was quickly discovering that my experiences in captivity had changed me. "I didn't really think about it before I went," I admitted to Marcus. "My fear for the kids who had crossed over before I did made me throw caution to the wind. I wanted to get them out. I didn't take time to weigh the consequences."

Yeah, maybe my actions *had* been reckless, but it had saved the teenagers.

If I had a choice of watching them die or risking a diversion by crossing over myself, I would do the same thing all over again.

"Think about the danger next time—before you act," he rumbled. "You scared the hell out of your entire family. Harper was beside herself, and your brothers were ready to cross the border to find you themselves, which would have gotten them all dead."

"It's not like I was *trying* to get kidnapped," I told him indignantly.

"Another few days of captivity probably would have killed you," Marcus answered rigidly.

"They were already talking about killing me," I confessed in a nervous tone, bringing up my captors for the first time all on my own.

"You understood them?"

I nodded as he turned his eyes to my face. "Yes. I speak some Arabic, but I never let on that I did. Since they weren't getting any money, there wasn't much reason for them to keep me alive. I guess I wasn't even any fun to play with anymore. I was too broken down to put up much of a fight."

"You look better," he said huskily, his tone slightly more gentle. "What did you do to your hair?"

I ran my fingers through the short pixie cut. "Nothing. The stylist just evened out the cut, and then dyed it all back to my natural color."

Being a detail guy, Marcus had sent me every service I needed while I was in the hospital, including somebody to fix my hair and try to heal all the cracks and breaks on my skin.

"You're a redhead?"

"Yes," I admitted. "But I thought I might have a better shot at the foreign correspondent job if I went blonde. Redheads draw a lot of attention, especially in foreign countries where that hair color is hardly ever seen. I wanted to blend in instead of standing out. I didn't really want anybody to know who I was."

Marcus seemed to be satisfied with my answer because he was silent for a few minutes. He wasn't a guy who spoke just to hear himself talking, a trait I was currently grateful he had.

Once the jet leveled off, I told Marcus, "I think I'll try to sleep for a while." I was exhausted from just the mild exercise I'd had during the day. All I'd really done was get discharged from the hospital and made my way to Marcus's jet. Still, I felt like I'd spent the entire day doing hard labor.

He opened his laptop computer, and without looking at me, he answered, "Bedroom is in the back. Go sleep as long as you want. It's a long trip."

"Thanks." I undid my seat belt and made my way to the back of the large aircraft.

My brothers all had private planes, so it wasn't unusual for me to see this level of comfort and convenience in a private jet. But it *did* feel strange to be the only other passenger in such a massive aircraft.

The sleeping area had a large king-sized bed, and a bathroom attached. I popped into the restroom to change into a nightgown. Seeing my suitcase next to the bedroom door had been no surprise. Marcus obviously demanded efficiency from his staff, and he got it without question.

"You done with the bathroom?" The sound of Marcus's voice beside me in the bedroom nearly made me jump out of my own skin. Yeah, I knew he was still on board, but he'd startled me.

Right now, it didn't take much to make me jumpy.

I nodded. The restroom had two entrances. One connected to the bedroom, and the other was right outside the bedroom door. A quick glance told me that the bathroom door next to the bedroom was closed, and Marcus was just politely checking to see if I was done.

I tried to calm my nerves, berating myself for being so damn jittery, and then looked up at Marcus to reassure him I wasn't a lunatic.

His sharp, ever-changing eyes were so intense that they felt like they were prying open my soul.

Without looking away from me, he answered, "I wanted to freshen up." He paused before asking, "Hey, are you okay? You're really pale."

"I-I'm fine," I lied easily.

In truth, I wasn't feeling well at all. My body was slowly getting stronger, but my mind wasn't functioning as well as it used to. I obviously startled easily, and I couldn't seem to keep my thoughts from returning to my time as a captive.

I'm safe. I'm safe.

I wondered if I kept up the mantra for a while, if I'd start to actually believe that nobody was going to hurt me.

"Bullshit," Marcus cursed. "You look like you can barely stand up."

He moved closer, his big body crowding me against the wall like he was ready to support me if I fell.

"I'm tired," I admitted as I continued to look up at him, trying not to react when he put a hand on each side of the wall, leaving me trapped.

"What else, Danica? What's bothering you? I know that look on your face. I've seen it before in other rescue situations."

Marcus was my only confidant at the moment, so I either told him what was wrong, or I kept it bottled up inside. I decided on the former. "I can't stop thinking about what happened. I was so damn certain I was going to die, Marcus. Returning to this world, knowing that I'm not going to be hurt again is pretty surreal. I'm happy. I really am. But the fear won't go away." The words tumbled out of my mouth awkwardly.

"That's normal," he told me. "You can't survive an ordeal like you went through without developing a heavy dose of worry and anxiety. Do you want to talk about it?"

Yes!

No!

Oh hell, I didn't know what I wanted. Maybe I *needed* to talk, but I certainly didn't want to, especially to Marcus. I was too used to always keeping my guard up around him. However, he was all I had right now.

"Not really," I murmured. "It's in the past. I just want to be myself again."

"I'm sorry we didn't get to you sooner," Marcus rumbled. "You were at those bastards' mercy for too damn long."

"You saved my life," I reminded him. "And it was a considerable risk for you and the rest of the rescue team. I'm just grateful you got there before I was dead."

Marcus lifted a hand to my face, and I automatically flinched. But he simply stroked over my bruised skin as he replied, "The assholes will pay for every damn time they touched you, Danica. I swear."

I shook my head. "I doubt they'll ever be found."

"They will," Marcus contradicted. "All of them are probably dead by now. The military was contacted the moment we moved out of the area so they could do an air strike on the compound." He paused before asking, "They're all dead. Does that help?"

Did it help to know that my tormentors were probably no longer alive? I wasn't certain it made a difference. "I don't know," I answered honestly. "They're still not dead in my mind, Marcus."

His touch was tender on my damaged skin, and his scent and warmth was intoxicating. Pretending I had Marcus to protect me helped. My mind was focused on him and the way he made me feel normal again.

"You'll stay safe, Dani. Nobody is going to hurt you again," he said with a feral growl.

Hesitantly, I wrapped my arms around his neck, shivering from just the casual contact of my fingers at the nape of his neck. "Thank you," I whispered, my gaze getting lost in his forceful gray stare.

His head came down slowly, giving me plenty of time to avoid him had I chosen to do so. But I *wanted* Marcus to touch me. I *wanted* to feel alive.

The embrace was gentle, a coaxing meeting of mouths, Marcus trying to cajole something out of me that he couldn't do with words.

He put his arms around me as he plundered my mouth, his hands stroking down my back and landing on my ass.

The second he pulled me forward, my scantily clad body colliding with his, I lost the sense of protection, heat, and tenderness in his kiss. His bold erection pressed against my lower abdomen, and I panicked, forgetting everything except my instinctive, visceral reaction.

My hands went to his chest, and I started to claw to get away from him. I tore my lips from his, unable to endure the flashes of memory that tore through my head. "No. Please. Don't."

"Dani!" Marcus said firmly, giving me a gentle shake. "What the hell happened? Open your eyes."

His commands finally sunk into my confused brain, and I opened my eyes. I hadn't even realized that I'd closed them to try to fend off the flashbacks, a spontaneous reaction that had just made them worse.

"Marcus?" His face was right there in my vision. "Oh, God. I'm sorry."

"Don't apologize for something that isn't your fault. I'm going to ask you one more time… Are you okay?"

Tears slid down my cheeks as I looked up at him. "No," I answered. "I don't think I *am* okay. Right now, I'm not sure I'll ever be normal again. I feel like a prisoner in my own body. It scares me."

"I know. Things will get better. But I can't help you if you don't want to talk about what happened." He hesitated, his eyes assessing my face. "You said you weren't sexually assaulted, but I think you're lying."

Breaking easily away from Marcus's hold, I swiped the tears from my face. "It's hard to talk about that period of time," I answered truthfully. "I was degraded, beaten down until I didn't even want to fight anymore. But I couldn't *not* try to fend them off. I don't want *anybody* to know everything that happened to me. I don't want to keep living it over and over again."

Every emotion I had seemed to have rocketed to the surface.

I continued, with my back to Marcus. "It was like a horrible nightmare that I couldn't escape even when I was awake. Especially while I was conscious and fairly alert. At first, it took several men to hold me down while I was raped. Eventually, they only needed a few. As I got weaker, I became easier and easier to use and torture."

"Why didn't you tell me?" Marcus answered sharply, turning me around to face him again.

My own fury became unleashed. "I didn't want to tell *anyone*. What difference would it make? It's not like they're going to be brought to justice in a court of law. My brothers would all want to kill the terrorists."

Marcus's expression was outrage. "Fuck that. I want to kill them just for touching you. Believe me, if they weren't already dead, I'd do the job myself."

I wrapped my arms around my own body to comfort myself. "Can you keep my secrets?" I asked in a raspy voice. "There's really no reason for anyone to know."

"You'll need counseling, Danica," Marcus answered hoarsely. "But yes, I can keep your secrets. What you tell people is completely up to you."

I sat down on the bed, my knees ready to give out from fear. I wanted to talk to somebody, but not my family. He was right. I probably would need therapy after what had happened, but I really didn't want to share this with my family. My sense of shame and humiliation was too raw. They all thought I was crazy to be running into turmoil and war zones. I didn't want them to know all the consequences of my job. All it would do was worry them when I eventually wanted to go back to work.

Marcus took off his suit jacket and tossed it over a small dresser in the room, and then took a seat in a chair near the bed. "I'm listening, Danica. Maybe you can't call me a friend, but I'm here to help if you need me."

He was composed, seemingly ready to hear about my experience.

The pain.

The terror.

The revulsion and humiliation I'd experienced when I was raped and beaten so often that I wasn't able to keep track of how many times it happened. And that once the rebels were finished with my body, how I'd wondered if *that time* would be the last.

I tried to swallow the lump in my throat as I glanced at Marcus's unreadable expression. Uncertain whether I could keep looking him in the eyes while I dumped my entire experience with the terrorists on him, I reached over and switched off the overhead light before I sat cross-legged in the middle of the bed.

Maybe I *couldn't* tell Marcus *every single detail* of my experience as a captive, but I knew I needed to vent and let some of my anger and fear exit my body by putting it all out in the open.

Satisfied that I couldn't see much of his expression in the dim light, I started to talk…

As promised, Marcus listened, occasionally letting me know that how I was feeling was perfectly natural considering what had happened.

By the time the flight was over, I'd collected myself and said a brief good-bye to the man who'd been my comfort and my confidant before I joined my sister in Washington, DC.

It would be a year before we met again, and he'd be responsible for stealing me away from somebody else one more time, but in very *different* circumstances...

Chapter 1

Marcus

The Present...

"What in the fuck am I doing here?" I muttered to myself irritably as I trudged down the crappy sidewalk in one of Miami's rougher areas.

The area was dimly lit, and the caliber of the neighborhood I was walking through had gone swiftly downhill. I hadn't been in Miami for a year or two, but it always amazed me that the affluent areas could abruptly end, and a short walk later, I'd end up in a dump.

Not that I gave a damn. I'd left my car and driver several blocks back, and in a better area. My elderly driver, George, didn't need to get his blood pressure up any higher, and I'd badly needed to clear my head with a walk before I met up with Danica.

I wasn't worried about my personal safety. I knew at least a hundred different ways to kill bad guys, and I was packing a loaded Glock under my suit jacket. If anybody wanted to screw with me, I'd make them sorry they were ever born. Hell, I'd actually welcome a decent fight right now. I was just that pissed off.

Dani and I had been in the same city a time or two in Europe, but we hadn't really seen each other. Okay, maybe I'd seen *her*, but she hadn't actually seen *me*. I'd known she was there because I'd made it a point to watch out for her and follow her work destinations. It hadn't really surprised me when she went back to reporting soon after she'd physically recovered. She was still in hot spots all over the world. The only place I *hadn't* seen her was the Middle East.

Then, a few months ago, I'd stopped seeing her altogether, and I hadn't been able to get much information about where she was going for her stories.

Now I knew why.

I'd been in Seattle a few days ago, and I'd dropped by Jett Lawson's place to see how he was recovering. Even though it had been a couple of years since Jett had nearly gotten killed on our last PRO mission together, he still required surgeries to repair some of his injuries. Most of the operations were cosmetic at this point, done to cover some of his scars. Unfortunately, thanks to his bitch of an ex-fiancée, some of Jett's emotional pain wasn't going to heal anytime soon.

But his own love life and ex-future marital partner hadn't been my buddy's concern when I stopped by to visit. Jett's thoughts had been diverted to his sister Danica's new boyfriend.

"Son of a bitch!" I cursed in an irritated voice as I approached the block where the bar I was seeking was located. "How in the hell did she get mixed up with a loser like Gregory Becker?"

Becker was a rich bastard, but it was doubtful that much of his wealth came from his legitimate businesses. He'd been a suspect at the CIA for a long time, but as of yet, nobody could make any charges stick with solid evidence or intel.

Stopping under a dim streetlamp, I pulled out the picture Jett had given me before I left Seattle, a photo that had been taken by a local newspaper in Miami. Dani had been captured in full color right next to Becker, his arm around her waist, both of them looking pretty damn happy at a charity event the asshole had donated to a few weeks ago.

There had been other photos, and other events where Dani had been by Becker's side. When Jett had asked Dani what she was doing in Miami, and if she was really seeing Becker, she'd told her brother that they were dating and it wasn't all that serious. Apparently, no matter what Jett had told his little sister, she'd refused to heed his warning about Becker. There probably wasn't a single wealthy businessman who didn't know Gregory Becker's reputation. Rumors were constantly flying about his involvement in human trafficking, illegal arms dealing, and a hell of a lot of drugs. He was also supplying much of that ill-gotten money to rebel troops in Syria. That little bit of info wasn't common knowledge. I'd learned that from some of the CIA intel.

How in the hell could Dani be mixed up with somebody who supplied money to rebel groups similar to the one who had held her captive and tortured the hell out of her?

Yeah, maybe Danica *wasn't* immersed in the world of international business, but she *had* to know about Becker. If she hadn't discovered his dirty secrets before, Jett certainly hadn't held back on telling her all about the new guy in her life. *Shit! Didn't she trust her own damn brother?*

Jett's concern for his little sister had brought me here to Miami when I had other places I should be. I kept telling myself that I wasn't here for me, but I knew I was bullshitting myself. For some reason, I'd never been able to forget the haunted look in Dani's eyes after her rescue and on the way home to the States.

Trying to kiss her on the jet had been an idiotic thing to do. Hell, even now, I don't know what had possessed me to touch her. But for some reason, I hadn't been able to stop myself.

Unfortunately, I hadn't known she'd been gang-raped over and over again. The way she had fought me, and the fact that I'd forced her into a full-blown panic, had left me feeling guilty ever since.

However, the moment before it had happened, the instant she'd trusted me before things had gotten out of control—the chemistry that had flared between us had haunted my ass, too.

I wasn't going to even pretend that what I felt for Dani was brotherly, and that I was completely here for Jett.

I'm here for myself, because I can't forget her.

Hell, for some reason, I hadn't even been able to be with another woman since I'd kissed Danica. How fucked up was that?

Not that I had *relationships,* but it would have been nice to have my healthy sex drive back again. One kiss and I'd practically been castrated. I hadn't made an effort to fuck any woman since I'd felt the silky softness of Dani's mouth beneath mine. The desire to get laid had been nonexistent. I was too obsessed with *her.*

I reminded myself that I wasn't *pursuing* her or any kind of relationship. I was just trying to save her ass…again.

The hair stood up at the back of my neck, and it pulled my mind from my fucked-up thoughts.

I shoved the picture back into my pocket and turned, already aware that I was being stalked.

It was almost disappointing that my would-be robber wasn't going to be much of a challenge.

He was all of maybe fourteen or fifteen years old, and didn't come anywhere close to my weight or my slightly-over-six-foot height.

The punk spoke in a voice that was meant to be menacing, but wasn't. Not to me. "Give me your wallet or I'll put this blade through your heart, mister."

Yeah, I'd been a walking target for robbery or mugging since I was strolling through a less than desirable area of Miami late at night in a custom suit. Still, this little prick was either bold or strung out on drugs if he thought I would just hand him my wallet. "Not happening," I drawled, annoyed. "Now beat it, kid."

He raised his arm in a threatening manner, wielding the knife wildly. "You think I'm a kid? I kill people like you every day, dude," he replied in a cocky tone.

If I ever laughed—which I didn't—I probably would have snickered. But I didn't show emotion—not ever. However, the youngster in front of me was rather amusing. He reminded me of an adolescent who had watched too many bad gangster movies.

I reached out, and in a split second I'd snatched his wrist, squeezing a nerve on his lower arm until he was forced to let go, and the weapon dropped onto the sidewalk with the loud clatter of steel meeting the cement. I pushed him into the cold metal of the streetlight pole, his face plastered against the post, and the Glock I'd previously kept concealed at his temple.

"That hurts," the kid griped nervously.

I leaned into his body and said close to his ear, "A bullet in your head would hurt a hell of a lot more. Go home, get off the drugs, and quit stealing from people to fund your habit."

"I live in a foster home," he protested, his voice anxious as I pushed the barrel of the gun into his temple just a little bit harder, hoping to scare the bejesus out of him.

"Then you're damn lucky to have a roof over your head," I growled. "Take advantage of it and quit being a little asshole. Keep this shit up and you'll be dead before you're legally able to drink."

I let go of him, but I put my foot over the knife on the ground before he could snatch it. "I said go home," I warned in an annoyed tone.

"Who the hell are you? I ain't seen you around on the streets," the kid asked hesitantly.

"Somebody you don't want to mess with," I answered vaguely.

The brat turned around and ran until he was out of my sight. I kicked the knife deep into the bushes next to the sidewalk, just in case he came back for it. I wasn't about to make it easy to find.

The boy was a bully, and I hated that. I probably should have called the cops and let them take him to jail, but I had bigger things to worry about. And although it was probably wishful thinking, maybe the punk would straighten himself out someday.

Problem was, he was obviously hooked on something. It wasn't hard to read the desperation of an addict. *Fucking hell!* I hated seeing a guy that young screwed up on drugs.

Shoving the gun back into its concealed holster, I pulled my jacket closed. I hadn't even taken the safety off. The kid might be a juvenile delinquent, but I still wasn't about to shoot a boy who probably wasn't old enough to vote. My only purpose had been to scare the shit out of him.

I brushed off my suit jacket because it was one of my favorites, and then proceeded to walk to the end of the block and to my destination.

When I arrived, I realized the bar was basically a dive, the neon sign in the window blinking like Christmas tree lights.

"Real fucking classy," I muttered to myself, unable to see Dani in this place.

However, this *was* where she was meeting up with Becker. *This sleazy bar was the best the jerk could do?* Danica was a goddamn Lawson, a woman who had more money than she could ever spend. And *this* is where the two lovebirds were trysting?

Jett had told me where his sister was going for the evening. I wondered if he knew that it was a haven for prostitutes and drug dealers.

Probably…not. My buddy would most likely lose it if he knew his little sister was hanging out in this dive.

I shook my head as I peered into the front window. If Jett *had* known, he'd have been here, even if he *was* recovering from his latest procedure. Dani's brother would have a damn heart attack if he knew she'd even set foot into this neighborhood and this shithole of a bar.

My eyes scanned the general layout of the small club from the large, very dirty window out front. I didn't see Becker, but I did finally spot a woman alone at the bar. Her hair color gave her away, the deep-red strands now long enough to brush her shoulders.

I grimaced as I noticed the short, black, leather skirt she was wearing, and the skimpy green top that barely covered her breasts. Her black stiletto heels were secured over the lower rung of the round stool, and she was sipping slowly on some fluffy drink that was topped with whipped cream.

"What in the hell are you doing, Danica? You sure as fuck don't belong here," I said in a raspy voice.

The clothes, the location, the boyfriend…everything was wrong. The Danica I was acquainted with wanted nothing more than to chase down a story that she thought needed to be told. She wore a T-shirt and jeans because it made it easier for her to go after her story.

She didn't wear several inches of makeup like she was sporting now.

She didn't need it.

She never had.

Dani Lawson was drop-dead gorgeous without makeup and with hair of whatever color she wanted to tint it.

Protective instincts rose up inside me, emotions I definitely didn't want but couldn't seem to contain.

Unlike Jett, my obsession to watch over Danica was far from platonic, even though I'd never fucked her.

As usual, my cock was standing at attention just from watching Dani sitting at the bar. She was my only weakness aside from my family, and I had a love/hate relationship with the youngest Lawson sibling because of it.

If I wanted to be truthful with myself—which I really didn't—I'd had blue balls for Dani almost from the first moment I met her. Maybe that's why we were always fighting before I'd rescued her in the Middle East. Of course, she *had* been under the false impression that I'd broken her older sister's heart. Or maybe it was because I was generally an asshole, and she had no problem standing up for herself. She was the only woman who'd never had a problem getting into my face if I pissed her off, and she'd actually made fun of me on occasion.

I definitely hadn't liked that, but I did grudgingly admire her for her outspoken, smart-ass demeanor.

I still remembered the stories she'd told about her captivity on our way back from Turkey to the US. That time, she'd been different from the woman I'd previously known. Her vulnerability had practically destroyed me because I knew how she'd been before being kidnapped.

My fists clenched in anger as I remembered her frightened, expressive eyes, and I wasn't sure how she'd even managed to survive the emotional and physical torture.

My eyes scanned the outside area of the club just to make sure that Becker wasn't arriving to meet Danica. Not that I really cared, but I wanted to be prepared if I was going to meet more resistance than just Dani's when I went to take her out of this place.

I'd promised Jett that I'd get his sister away from danger, and this place reeked of evil. Dani didn't belong here, and whatever crazy bullshit Becker was feeding her needed to be cut off now.

As I stepped up to the glass door, I saw a drunken patron sidle up to the bar, using the stable surface to keep him upright.

"Don't touch her. Don't you fucking touch her," I growled as I yanked the door open.

Danica's squeal of alarm rang through the rancid air of the bar just as I stepped inside.

There was a male hand on Dani's ass that didn't belong to me, and anybody touching her *there* who *wasn't* me was completely unacceptable. The trashed male was twice her size, and as his fingers curled around her wrist to try to drag her off the barstool, I lost total control of my reasoning ability. It was something that had never happened to me before, but as I stepped forward, it felt pretty damn good to plant my fist in his face and watch him hit the dirty floor with a satisfying *thud*.

Chapter 2

Dani

I hated this bar.
   I hated this area.
   I hated the hooker skirt and top I was wearing.
And I *really* hated the sickly sweet drink I was sipping.

However, I also wanted to see Greg Becker, and I knew he'd arrive here eventually. He was habitually late for almost everything, so I knew I'd have to be patient.

"Hey, little lady," a tall, drunk man said to me as he stumbled to the bar. "A sweet thing like you shouldn't be alone. How much?"

My skin crawled as the guy's hand squeezed the cheek of my ass through my tight leather skirt, and his face moved so close to mine that I could smell his rotten breath.

I should expect to be propositioned. I'm in a bar where most of the women are prostitutes. This is where they get most of their hookups.

Nevertheless, I let out a squeamish scream as the cheek of my butt got palmed and squeezed even harder.

"Not for sale," I said in a warning voice, ready to forcibly remove his hands from my body. He was so drunk that he'd probably fall over if he didn't have any support.

I never got the opportunity to test my theory and shake off his grip. One very large fist to the drunk's face and he toppled like a ton of bricks.

I jerked my head to the left to see who had rescued me.

Then I took a second look.

Marcus? What in the hell was he doing here?

"Let's go," he grumbled as he clasped my hand and pulled me awkwardly off the barstool.

I stumbled over the unconscious man at my feet, barely avoiding putting a stiletto in his privates. "I can't leave. I'm meeting someone," I protested.

"Not anymore," he answered in a graveled voice.

I was already outside the door when I dug my heels in, trying to yank my hand from his. Marcus was wicked strong, and I'd be compelled to keep moving if he kept dragging me along. "What are you doing here?" I asked breathlessly, stopping him temporarily, but still unable to break his grip.

"Taking your ass back to where you belong."

"I belong *here*. I have a date, Marcus. I can't just leave. I need to see Greg."

"Didn't anything Jett told you sink in?" Marcus replied stiffly. "Becker is an asshole and a goddamn criminal."

"I heard Jett. I just didn't agree," I said huffily. "I'm old enough to decide who to go out with, for God's sake."

"Not if you're making the wrong choices," he replied in a clipped voice.

I both loved and hated his arrogant voice. The tone, the confidence, and the blunt, no-nonsense inflections in the deep baritone were uniquely Marcus Colter, but the things he said annoyed me to no end.

I yanked on my imprisoned hand again, but couldn't free myself. Marcus had a tight grip on me, but he wasn't hurting me. "And who are you to decide if my choices are right or wrong?"

"They're wrong," he said flatly. "Let's move."

I had to either stumble along behind him or go face-first into the pavement. Since I was a survivor, I followed him.

I cursed myself for sharing so much with my brother, Jett. He'd obviously sent Marcus in his place since he disapproved of me seeing Becker. I hadn't expected that, nor did I want it.

"Marcus, I have to go back," I argued. "Greg will be at his bar any minute."

"He owns that shithole?" he asked without slowing his pace.

"It's not that bad," I lied. "It's a friendly, local place."

"Yeah. Just one big happy family of criminals and hookers," he rasped.

"Not everyone is born rich," I shot back at him as I worked to keep pace with his long stride.

"No. They aren't. But Becker is rich. The bastard doesn't need you to meet with him there, and he could keep you out of his dishonest endeavors."

I was silent for a moment before I replied, "What makes you think he's dishonest?"

He slowed down a little as he turned his head toward me and grimaced. "Apparently, you're the only one who *doesn't* know he's a crook, and a traitor to his own damn country."

I ignored his accusations. "Stop. Please. I have to go back."

"We're getting the hell out of here, and then you're going to tell me how exactly you two got together in the first place."

"I can't go with you." I started struggling hard to free myself from Marcus. I twisted my arm, hoping he'd be forced to let go of my hand.

"Stop. You'll injure yourself," he demanded.

"I'm not going with you," I argued.

"Yeah, you are," he insisted.

A startled scream exited my mouth as Marcus bent over, lifted my body off the ground, and threw me over his shoulder.

I pounded on his back, fairly certain my ass was probably hanging out of the short skirt I was wearing. "Put me down," I said, angry now that he was carrying me like a caveman.

His rock solid body bearing my weight effortlessly, he moved in long strides that ate up distance rapidly, ignoring my protests. The only thing I could see—unless I strained my neck—was the back of his suit jacket.

Dammit! This couldn't happen. I *had* to be at the bar!

"Hello, George. We're ready to go back to the penthouse," I heard Marcus say to somebody I couldn't see.

"Yes, sir," the other man—obviously named George—replied, his voice not betraying a single iota of alarm that his boss had come back to the vehicle with a woman slung over his shoulder.

"Ooooff!" The air was forced out of my lungs as my back landed against the soft leather of a car seat. My head was spinning as I tried to get my bearings, suddenly upright again after being carried upside down.

Marcus entered on the other side of the car, taking up the vacant space in the backseat beside me.

The vehicle was in motion before my head cleared.

"Dammit!" I cursed, pushing the hair back from my face as I straightened myself up in the seat. "Do you understand that you just pretty much kidnapped me?"

"You left me very little choice," Marcus replied nonchalantly.

I took a deep breath and let it out slowly, trying to calm my nerves. "You had a choice. You could have just left me alone. I'm a grown woman. I've traveled the world alone. I can make my own damn choices."

I still couldn't figure out why Marcus was even in Miami, and at Greg's bar. The only reason I could come up with was my brother.

"Jett was concerned," he confirmed.

I sighed. The last thing I wanted was for my youngest brother to be upset. Jett had been through so damn much, and he deserved a little bit of peace. "He doesn't need to worry. I'm all grown up. I have been for years."

"Why are you here, Danica? What happened to your career? You haven't been outside of the US for months now," he asked in a graveled voice.

I didn't lie to him. "I needed a break. The places where I really needed to be—I just couldn't go to right now."

After what had happened to me, I'd needed some serious counseling, and I still wasn't done going to therapy. I wasn't able to go back to reporting in the Middle East without fear, and that had always been my beat. It was a fear I hadn't been able to conquer, so I'd finally given the network my notice and struck out on my own to work as an independent journalist. My sister, Harper, thought I'd pushed too hard to go back to work, and maybe she was partly right, but my kidnapping had irrevocably changed me. I'd *never* be the same woman I was before I'd been taken as a hostage.

"You should take as much time off as you need. Nobody expected you to bounce back and be working again."

"I wanted the distraction. I couldn't stand being alone with my own thoughts," I admitted. "But I couldn't do it. I'm not the same person anymore, and I'm not quite sure who I am."

Marcus spoke hoarsely in the dark interior of the vehicle. "You're still the same, Dani. Inside, you haven't changed. You're just seeing the world around you differently."

I leaned my head back against the headrest, wondering if what Marcus said was true. Maybe I hadn't changed. Maybe he was right. Maybe I just couldn't look at the world with the same innocence that I used to. "I hope so," I answered wistfully.

"You aren't going to find whatever you need with Gregory Becker," he warned.

"I don't know that yet," I told him firmly. "I don't even know him that well."

"You don't need to know him any better," Marcus answered stiffly.

"You don't understand," I told him in a shaky voice.

"Then please enlighten me," he suggested drily. "Because I can't see the appeal of someone like him." He hesitated before asking, "Did you fuck him?"

"What?" I wasn't sure I'd heard him correctly.

"Did. You. Fuck. Him?" His voice was husky and grim.

"No!" The word shot out of my mouth without censoring my response. "Not that it's any of your business who I sleep with," I added.

"I'm making it my business."

"Because of Jett," I guessed.

"No. Because I risked lives to save your ass. I didn't do it so you could throw that life away on a loser like Gregory Becker."

"It's *my* life," I snapped at him. Marcus was making everything difficult.

"Break it off," he commanded. "Do you really want to marry a man like him? Jesus, Dani, he's a criminal. He just hasn't gotten caught yet. But he will. And you'll be caught in the middle of the entire mess, or dead because of his enemies. He doesn't give a damn about you. If he did, he wouldn't want you to wait in a bar filled with drunks and prostitutes."

"I'm not marrying him," I said angrily. "I'm just dating him. That's all."

"No more dates. No more meeting him at his bar. No more anything. Tell him you've lost interest and move on," Marcus drawled.

"Stop!" I suddenly hollered at the driver. Surprisingly, he brought the limo to a halt.

"What are you doing, Danica?" Marcus reached over and grabbed my wrist.

I shook off his hold. "I'm home. My condo is in the building right behind us."

"I didn't know you had a place here."

"I didn't know you did, either," I told him as I opened the car door. "But apparently you do."

My neighborhood was well lit, but I still couldn't see Marcus's expression as he leaned over the backseat. "My place is close, so I'll be around. This is a decent area. Just stay out of Becker's turf."

I closed the door without answering, and then scrambled to the stairs of my condo building as fast as my high stilettos would take me there.

Marcus didn't get out of the car, but he didn't leave until I'd made it past security and ducked into the building.

By the time I got to my condo and looked out the window, Marcus was gone.

Marcus

"Since when does Danica have a condo here in Miami?" I asked Jett, using the speakerphone on my cell so my hands were free and I could yank off my tie.

The luxury penthouse I owned had walls of windows with spectacular beachside views when it was daylight. But since it was dark, there was every possibility that some neighbor could see me stripping down to my underwear, but I didn't give a shit.

It was summer, and it was pretty damn hot and humid in Southern Florida. I wanted to get my dirty clothes off. I grudgingly admitted that I also needed to give my poor dick a break. I'd been rock-hard since the moment I'd seen Danica in that skimpy blouse and tight leather skirt. Unfortunately, I hadn't been able to get that image out of my mind since she'd jumped out of my limo with her ass barely covered.

"Actually, she and Harper own the condo," Jett informed me. "They both love the beach."

I yanked my tie loose and dropped it on a chair. "She's at her condo for now," I said, starting on the buttons of my shirt. "But

I'm not sure she'll stay there. I just can't figure out what's so damn appealing about Becker."

"I'm not sure," Jett mused. "All I know is that Dani has been different since she came back from her kidnapping."

"Different how?"

"This might sound weird, but she seems…sad. She used to be able to have more fun than any of us. Now I never even see her smile anymore."

Come to think of it, I hadn't seen her smile, either. Granted, we'd both been working when we'd met up in the past, but that hadn't stopped her from smiling and laughing before. She'd always been feisty, but she seemed more like a shadow of that woman now. Not that she wasn't still sassy, but she had a harder edge. "She was going to be changed, Jett. You can't go through an experience like Danica did without coming away from the experience a changed person."

I didn't tell him that Dani had already explained that she *felt* different, that she wasn't sure who she was anymore.

For some reason, that bothered me. Danica *was* the same person inside, but she seemed incredibly…wary. She looked at the world as a different, much scarier place. Although I understood why she felt that way, I detested the fact that she was no longer able to look at places and people with the same curiosity she used to have.

Even though she had a wickedly sharp mouth, the innocence she'd once had was gone, and I mourned the loss. It made me feel even more protective and determined to make sure she regained the sense of wonder that had been so much a part of her before.

"Maybe everything we've heard about Becker is just rumor," Jett contemplated aloud. "What if he's actually a decent guy? I'd feel like a jerk if I tried to take somebody away from Dani who she cared about if the only thing he's guilty of is being the subject of rumors."

With the buttons free, I yanked off my shirt and tossed it onto the same chair where my tie had landed.

What in the hell could I tell Jett? Nobody except my family knew that I worked as a special operative for the CIA. I *couldn't* explain that the agency had been trying to gather intel on Becker for years, and that one day they'd get what they needed to put him away. He was the worst of the worst, a guy who got rich on making people into addicts and prostitutes, and it wasn't always by their choice. I was fairly certain the suspicion of Becker funding the terrorists was true. We just hadn't been able to find the intel that linked him, without doubt, to the rebels.

"No chance of that," I finally answered. "He's an asshole."

"I hate being fucking lame," Jett said in a frustrated tone. "I'd like to be there with you right now. But I have another minor surgery tomorrow. All this work to try to make me look presentable again. Hell, I know some of these marks will never heal, and I'll always probably limp when I'm tired."

I could almost hear his irritation through the phone connection, and as usual, I felt guilty as hell. "I wish I'd never brought you into PRO."

"I don't regret it, Marcus. We did a lot of good things, saved a lot of lives. And in the end, I didn't end up married to a woman who only wanted my money. But even *she* couldn't tolerate my injuries, even if it would make her wealthy as hell."

I flinched as I stepped out of my pants, tossed them on the chair, and then flopped onto a white leather couch, dressed only in a pair of boxer briefs. "You made a lucky escape from that one," I agreed. "But I feel like shit because I brought you into PRO. It was my operation."

Jett had been in the wrong place at the wrong time. When our helicopter had gone down, anybody who was on the side that bit the dust had some crush injuries from heavy equipment and other supplies falling on top of them. Jett had gotten the worst of it. He'd been on the wrong side *and* in the wrong area. I'd only suffered minor injuries, something I'd felt guilty as hell about seeing as a few on my team had been injured way worse. The others had recovered, but Jett would never be quite the same, and that ate at me.

For some time, his internal injuries had been so bad that nobody knew if he would make it. When we realized he was going to live, we discovered it wasn't happening without challenges. They'd put my buddy and team member back together, but his leg would never be the same, and he had a lot of scarring.

"I wouldn't do it any differently, even if I could," Jett answered thoughtfully. "Besides, you needed me. I'm the best damn tech intel guy you could get."

I let out a bark of laughter—which was unusual for me—but I knew what he was saying was true. I owed many of PRO's successful missions to Jett. He was a damn genius when it came to Internet technology and programming.

I stood up and went to the fridge for a beer, screwing the top off as I answered, "You got me there. There's nobody better in the field."

"Damn right," Jett quipped.

"What are you working on now?" I asked curiously.

"Not much," he answered glumly. "Haven't had a lot of time. But the current projects for the company are progressing well."

Jett owned an enormous computer technology and cyber security company, and was doing a number of projects at any given time. Luckily, his profession was something he could manage at home in Seattle.

"Just worry about recovering," I told him. "I think you're rich enough."

"Not as loaded as you are," he protested. "But it's never been about the money for me anyway."

Jett's father and mother had died in a car accident, leaving all of their children with billions of dollars, much like what had happened to my father. "But you're doing what you love," I answered.

"Aren't you doing what you love, Marcus?"

I took a slug of my beer before I dropped back onto the sofa. I didn't mind running my father's multinational conglomerate, but I couldn't say it was really my passion. "I didn't have a lot of choice. Once my father died, I had to step up to the plate as soon as possible. I was the oldest."

Once we'd lost our dad, I'd felt compelled to take care of my father's legacy. Unfortunately, once I was old enough, dealing with my dad's conglomerate couldn't be accomplished without a hell of a lot of travel. We'd had management in place until I finished school, but the company hadn't been as solid as it had been when my father had been alive. So I'd traveled, making sure things were done the right way, handling all of the problems myself.

Except, sometimes I felt like by doing right with the company, I'd somehow lost track of my family. Having been gone so much, there were so many things I'd missed. Chloe had been in an abusive relationship, and I hadn't discovered it until after she was out of it. I'd slowly drifted away from my identical twin, Blake, who was now a US Senator. Tate and Zane had been through their own hardships, too, and once again, I hadn't been there for them very much.

Truth was, I missed them like hell, but because I'd been absent for so long, I wasn't sure how to be back in their lives again. Considering my work with the CIA, maybe it was for the best.

"Well, it's not like you don't have time to pursue anything you want to," Jett finally answered.

Right now, the only thing I wanted to *pursue* was his gorgeous, stubborn, redheaded sister. But I couldn't tell him that.

"Yeah," I agreed noncommittally. "I'll hang out here for at least a few more days and keep an eye on Dani. I want to make sure she doesn't cozy up to Becker again."

Jett was quiet for a moment before he said, "You know, if she does, there isn't much we can do, short of kidnapping her. I want to protect her, but she deserves her space. If she wants him, I can't exactly stop her."

"I *will* stop her," I grumbled, purposely not mentioning I'd already technically kidnapped Danica. "She'd fuck up her entire life if she ends up with Becker. He'll go down eventually."

"You okay, Marcus?" Jett asked carefully.

"Yeah. Why?"

"I guess I've never really seen you take a personal matter this seriously."

"Just trying to help," I told him awkwardly.

He was right. Very rarely did I give much thought to personal stuff that didn't involve my businesses or CIA intel.

She was my downfall when it came to being emotionally distant. Danica had been through so much, not to mention the fact that I had some kind of odd, animalistic possessiveness toward her that I couldn't explain or understand. For a very long time, all I'd wanted was to get her naked, and then pin her against the wall while we both got our fill of each other. And I was pretty certain it would take me one hell of a long time to get rid of the primitive drive I harbored to make Danica mine. I wanted to fucking hear her scream that she belonged to me while I pounded into her tight, warm heat.

However, after she'd shared some of the pain she'd had to bear during her confinement with the rebels, I was driven to make sure she never suffered again.

"Let me know how it goes," Jett requested. "And thanks, man. I owe you one."

We ended our call, and I stood up, restless from being at loose ends for the first time I could remember. I'd asked one of my top executives to fill in on my travel for me, and I'd headed for Florida specifically to let Dani know that she couldn't keep seeing Becker.

Something isn't right. I can feel it.

My logical brain was telling me that there was no way she wanted Gregory Becker. Dani was too damn smart to end up with a man like him. Not only that, but she was a reporter, a woman who could read people extremely well.

Meanwhile, my irrational, primal, carnal response wanted to move Dani completely out of harm's way immediately and completely.

I wish I could say that my logical mind was going to seek out answers, but I was afraid that for the first time in my life, I might very well be unable to completely ignore emotion.

Chapter 4

Dani

The following day, I'd had to make up an excuse for Greg as to why I wasn't at the bar to meet him.

I really wanted him to trust me, so letting him down like that wasn't exactly a step forward for our relationship.

Fortunately, he'd accepted the fact that I hadn't been feeling well and had fallen asleep. The really bad part was that he wanted to come over and see me here at my condo to make sure I was feeling better.

He thinks I'm sick. He probably won't stay long.

I'd dressed in a pretty, casual, yellow sundress, and then put on some makeup. I left my hair down in a sleek bob that barely touched my shoulders. Somehow, the style seemed to fit my natural red-headed color.

My phone rang, and I hurried to unplug the cell phone on the living room coffee table so I could answer before the caller got my voice mail. "Hello," I answered. I hadn't looked at the caller ID, so I was half expecting the call to be from Greg, saying he was going to be late or that he had to cancel his visit.

"Dani?" a panicked female voice asked in a nervous tone.

"Ruby? What's the matter? What happened?" I asked breathlessly. I stressed out over my young friend on a daily basis. After a childhood and adolescence of abuse, she'd ended up running away and had landed in Miami at the age of eighteen. She'd been here and homeless for almost four years, a fact I hadn't learned about until after she was picked up off the street right after we'd met a month or two ago. She had a home in a crappy hotel room now, but everything about the arrangement that had taken her off the streets worried me.

"The guy who rescued me says I owe him. This isn't what I thought it would be, Dani. They promised me I'd have a job, and that hasn't happened. Now they're telling me I owe money for the roof over my head and food. Since I don't have money to pay them back, they want to do some kind of auction thing for my services."

My stomach rolled as I thought about just what kind of auction Ruby was going to participate in. "Did they say what kind of auction?"

"T-They didn't s-say," she stammered. "But the woman who comes to bring me food asked if I was a virgin, and I admitted that I was. At first, I was thinking some kind of live-in housekeeper or something. But I'm starting to think they want me to sell my body since it's really all I have to give."

I breathed in deeply and then blew the air out. I had been pretty certain that whoever had picked her up had expected to somehow profit from helping Ruby. It was a situation ripe for human trafficking. "Did they say when?" I asked, trying not to sound as concerned as I felt.

"N-No. I think they want to put some weight on me first. Dani, I'm so scared. I know I have a place to stay and food to eat now, but I almost wish I was homeless again. I racked up debt with these people, and I have to pay them back."

God, I desperately wanted to move Ruby to my condo and make sure nobody harmed her ever again. But I had a few reasons why that wasn't possible at the moment. "Hang in there. I promise I'll get you out of there before anything happens."

"I got myself into a bad situation, didn't I?" she asked.

"Yes. But it's not your fault. These people aren't taking women and kids off the streets to help them. I think they're human traffickers." I shuddered at the thought of how many other women had been subject to their "kindness."

"I don't know what to do. They said if I try to leave without paying my debt, they'll find me," she whimpered.

"We'll take care of it. Stay strong, Ruby. Ask them how much you owe."

"Whatever it is, I can't pay it without a job," she answered flatly.

"I know you don't know me that well, but can you trust me?" I questioned desperately.

Ruby hesitated for a moment before replying, "It's hard for me to trust anybody," she said honestly. "But I'll try. You've already helped me a lot just by being a friend. I'm not as afraid now that I know that somebody knows and cares about me."

"I'll get you out," I promised. "Just keep me updated on what's happening when you safely can."

"I will. Thank you."

It broke my heart to hear her so sad and frightened. But she really had never had anything to be happy about. Her twenty-two years of life had been pretty damn harsh.

We ended our call, but my gut was still tied up in painful knots when I hung up the phone. Really, I'd been a wreck ever since I'd seen Marcus at Greg's bar. Our encounter had been unsettling, especially when I realized that just seeing him again had reminded me of every wet dream I'd ever had about him.

And I'd had too many to count.

I'd been pretty confused and wounded after Marcus had rescued me, but the mysterious pull that drew me to him was just as present as it had been when he'd risked his ass to pull me out of Syria. Honestly, I'd been drawn to him almost from the beginning of our acquaintance. The difficulty was, I now knew exactly what I was feeling. I was incredibly attracted to Marcus, and I had no idea how to stifle it.

The chemistry had always been there, but I hadn't been able to acknowledge the desire right after I'd escaped my kidnappers. But I'd had plenty of therapy to help me start to move on from that horrific experience, and I was able to admit that something about Marcus made me completely crazy. He was definitely hot, so wanting to have him pin me up against the wall and satisfy me wasn't surprising. I guess it was all the other emotions that seemed to get tangled up with my passionate desire to screw him that baffled me.

I admired what he'd been doing with PRO, even though my brother had been injured in one of the missions. Marcus always seemed to have everything under control in a way I'd never seen before. Granted, he'd gotten arrogant and bossy with me, but there was still some kind of nerves of steel that he seemed to carry along with him as easily as other men carried their cell phones. I'd seen him in plenty of hot spots, but he'd never seemed to be aware of the danger of being there. Hell, I wasn't sure I'd ever seen a wrinkle in his custom suit when he was doing business in all of the war-torn areas of the world where we'd collided.

I'd *had* to be in the scariest areas of the world for my job, but really, Marcus had never *had* to be in those places at all. Strangely, he just treated his travels like everyday work obligations, no matter where he happened to be.

"But what is he doing here in Miami?" I mumbled to myself as I sat on the arm of the couch to wait for Greg.

And why is he so concerned about who I'm dating?

Yeah, he said Jett was concerned, but Marcus wasn't the type of guy to be somewhere he didn't want to be.

Our entire encounter at Greg's bar had been baffling. I'd never seen Marcus in anything but work mode except during his dangerous rescue and the short time we'd spent together afterward. Acting like he was *personally* concerned was disconcerting.

I tried to shrug it off. It didn't matter if he liked Greg or not. He'd have to deal with the fact that I was dating somebody he didn't think was a good match for me. Nobody had ever interfered in my love life, and it wasn't happening now. My relationship with Greg was too important to me.

The doorbell finally rang, and I shook myself out of my negative thoughts to go answer the door.

"Hello, gorgeous," Greg drawled as I opened the door.

"Hi," I answered breathlessly.

He kissed me on the cheek and then walked into the living room as I closed the door.

"How are you feeling?" he questioned, making himself at home as he took a seat on the couch.

"Better," I replied, hoping he didn't grill me about not showing up at the bar for our date.

Greg was the type of man who was always cautious, always careful. He was attractive and fit, and had a nice, thick head of blond hair that would send most women running after him, even if he wasn't filthy rich. But there was a veil over his dark eyes that would never quite let anybody in.

My goal was to know him better than any woman ever had, and teach him to trust me. Unfortunately, me not showing at his bar—or so he thought—probably made him nervous. Greg was always watching for any kind of reaction or anything that didn't fit into his world exactly the way he thought it should. Me being absent last night shouldn't make him paranoid, but I'd already discovered that with Greg, any odd behavior was suspect.

"I'm glad," he finally answered, his eyes raking over me like he wanted to see if I was telling the truth.

"Would you like a drink?" I asked politely.

"No, gorgeous. I just came to make sure you were...safe."

I sat down on the couch next to him. We'd only been on a few dates, and attended a few charity events together. The most intimacy we'd experienced was a kiss at the door. "Maybe I was just tired," I lied.

"I thought you were sick," he said, sounding suspicious.

I shook my head. "I was, but maybe I just felt that way because I didn't get enough sleep."

He reached out and took my hand, squeezing it tighter than needed to show simple affection. "Then you should get some rest, Dani."

"I will," I replied, trying not to notice that my hand was losing circulation from his hold.

"I don't really like the fact that you stood me up last night. But I'll get over it," he said in a warning voice, a tone that told me that I'd better never do it again.

"I'm really sorry," I answered remorsefully.

"I'm powerful in this city, Dani. A man like me doesn't have to wait."

"I know," I agreed.

Gregory *was* a force to be reckoned with in Miami. He was extremely rich, and donated money to politicians and law enforcement to keep them indebted to him. He didn't have the power of a Lawson or a Colter, but his multimillionaire status made him a VIP in all of South Florida.

He stood up, pulling me to my feet because of his grip on my hand. "I'm glad you understand me," he answered with a smirk.

"Are you leaving already?" I questioned, looking up at him with a tremulous smile.

"I have things to do," he affirmed. "But I had to check on you."

"Thank you," I said.

He pulled me against him and dropped a kiss on my mouth before he answered, "I had to make sure you knew how I felt about not seeing you at my club last night."

His emotions were pretty crystal-clear, actually. Greg was a control freak, and anything he couldn't make go his way wasn't acceptable.

"I won't let you down again," I promised.

"That's good. Very good," he answered as he finally let go of my hand. "Stay healthy, Dani. I want to see you in my bed as soon as you're feeling better."

I wanted to shake my hand to return the circulation to my extremity, but I didn't.

His announcement about wanting to have sex with me wasn't a surprise. He'd made it perfectly clear when we'd met that he wanted me.

And I was pretty certain that up until last night, he'd always gotten what he wanted.

I followed him to the door and saw him out, leaning against the wood after I'd flipped the bolt.

"That didn't go exactly the way I'd hoped," I whispered to myself as I blew out a breath that I hadn't realized I'd been holding.

Greg would never be a warm and fuzzy kind of guy. He had an extremely hard edge to him that should make me want to run away from him as quickly as possible. But I didn't because I really wanted to get close to him.

I straightened and pushed myself off the door, starting to feel as exhausted as I told Greg I'd been the night before.

"How do I get close to him when he never lets his guard down?" I mused aloud as I walked to the kitchen.

Greg hadn't told me when he wanted to meet again, but I knew there would be more dates, more time spent together, and I'd do everything in my power to try to be his confidant.

I refused to accept that our relationship would go any other way.

Chapter 5

Marcus

"Son of a bitch!" I cursed as I saw Gregory Becker leave Dani's apartment.

I was sitting in the parking lot near Danica's condo in my luxury rental car, doing surveillance. It was difficult for me to force myself not to go after the little weasel.

Had the bastard hurt Dani?

What was he doing at her place?

I'd spent plenty of time thinking about Dani and Becker together, but my gut still hurt every time I thought about Becker laying a hand on her.

Why in the fuck am I sitting in her parking lot alone, watching her condo?

I took a deep breath and let it out as I watched that dickhead Becker get into his presumptuous luxury sports car and leave. I couldn't approach him. Not yet. I needed more information, which answered my question as to why I was watching Dani's condo.

Somehow, I'd known that Becker would show up.

And I was, after all, a goddamn spy. Being patient and collecting information was what I did. And I was very good at doing that.

I just didn't like it very much right now, especially not the *being patient* part of the task.

I didn't want to wait.

I wanted to confront the asshole right fucking now.

There was no question as to whether or not I was going to check up on Dani. If Becker had been at her place, I wanted to make sure she was safe. At least that was how I rationalized driving closer to her condo, getting out of my vehicle, and making my way to the entrance of her condo building.

There was minimal security at the entrance, and it wasn't difficult to gain entry by simply following another occupant through the door once they'd entered the code.

It hadn't been hard to get all the information on Dani that I'd wanted once I'd requested a file on her from DC. And yeah, I'd rationalized *that* action too, telling myself I needed her address and any other recent information I could get because she was dating somebody who was on the radar of the federal government. Hell, I'd been sent a loaded file of information, but none of it was all that relevant to her current status as Becker's love interest.

I grimaced as I rang her doorbell, the thought of Becker so much as touching a hair on Dani's head making my gut churn.

She's one of my best friend's sisters. It isn't abnormal for me to be concerned.

Really, I pretty much knew that excuse was bullshit, but I let it roll off my back. Danica Lawson was off-limits, even if I did get hard every time I saw her. She always had been. Dani *was* Jett's sister, and I absolutely couldn't just nail her without everything becoming complicated. And I hated complications. Now that I had my priorities straight, I was determined to keep a level head.

"What are you doing here?" Dani asked, her voice disapproving as she stared at me from the door she'd just opened.

Christ! Didn't she bother to ask who was ringing her doorbell before she just opened the door that way? "You never answered all my questions," I replied, inviting myself into her home as I brushed past her.

"I don't need to explain myself to you," she said huffily before she closed the door, turned toward me and then crossed her arms stubbornly. "You need to leave. I doubt that Greg is always watching me, but I don't want him to know you were here."

"Do you do everything he tells you to do?" I remarked as calmly as possible. "Doesn't it concern you even a little bit that you aren't sure whether or not some guy is watching you?"

Hell, it worried *me* that Danica might be in deep enough with Gregory Becker that he might have put somebody on her to watch her every move. She should be terrified.

"No. It doesn't bother me." She eyed me suspiciously as she added, "I see you lost the custom suit today."

"It's Saturday," I answered. "I don't wear a suit on the weekends."

She snorted. "It's good to know you lighten up two days out of the week."

I frowned at her. "I don't ever *lighten up*. I just dress more relaxed."

Danica looked beautiful in a casual yellow dress that made her hair appear to be a deeper red. And if I appeared more lax than usual, it was because of my father. He'd always tried to be with his kids on the weekends, and he lost the suit on Saturday and Sunday when he was home, and tried to just be our dad. For some reason, I always followed his example, even though I didn't have anybody who cared what I wore. But it made me somehow feel like I was following in his footsteps when I wore jeans and a casual shirt when it wasn't a workday.

My weekend attire did make it difficult to pack a gun. But I managed.

"It's a good look on you," she answered as she moved closer, and looked up at me with an irritated expression. "But what *are* you doing here, Marcus? I still haven't forgotten the fact that you literally hauled me away from a date."

"Get over it," I suggested. "Since you're affiliating with somebody who is possibly guilty of international crimes, you needed to be taken away from trouble."

"What do you mean?"

"Gregory Becker has been rumored for years to be into some unsavory ways of making money. It isn't a secret in the business world."

"They're just rumors," she said defensively.

"Behind every rumor is a grain of truth," I warned. "You know that. How did you ever get tangled up with somebody like him? And what happened to your job as an international correspondent?"

Her eyes left my face as she turned around and sat on the arm of her couch. "I told you I needed a break. I lost my edge," she admitted hesitantly. "I worked around Europe and other countries, but I never could manage to go back to the Middle East without panicking. I decided to leave my network."

I saw a look of vulnerability flash across her face. Generally, I could find a way to use that moment of weakness to my advantage, but I didn't have the stomach for it with Danica. "That's understandable after what happened to you."

She shook her head. "As a reporter, I couldn't afford to be afraid. My neurosis could endanger my whole crew. But I wasn't fearless anymore. I haven't been the same since…the incident."

Dani had reason to want to stay as far away from the location of her kidnapping as possible. She wouldn't be human if she *wasn't* wary. "You could have stayed on as an European correspondence."

"I needed something different," she said, her eyes trained away from mine. "I just wanted some time."

"Then take all the time you need. It was madness to go back so soon after what happened." I hesitated before asking, "What part of the hostage situation is still haunting you?"

I wasn't sure I could deal with her answer without wanting the bastards who'd kidnapped her to be alive again so I could snuff them out myself. Oh yeah, Dani had talked to me, but I had a feeling she was leaving out a very large chunk of what had happened to her.

"What does it matter?" she asked. "It's not like they'll ever serve time or pay for what happened to me."

"They can't be because they're all dead," I informed her flatly. She already knew that, but I felt compelled to remind her that none of the rebels would ever bother her again. Personally, I felt like instant death was something they hadn't deserved.

Her head jerked back toward me, and her expression was solemn. "Logically, I understand that, but my brain isn't always reasonable, Marcus. How did you ever get that information? You never told me how you knew. The information should have been classified."

I could hardly tell her that I had quite a lot of intel from the government. Nobody knew about my involvement with the CIA and intelligence gathering except my family. Not even her brother, Jett. My PRO team had only known that I was skilled in private rescue operations. "I overheard a conversation about it," I lied smoothly because I was accustomed to twisting the truth.

Her expression changed as tears began to flow down her cheeks. "Is it terrible to say that I'm glad they're all dead?" she questioned, her body visibly shaking.

"Of course not," I said. "After what happened, you should be glad they're off the face of the earth."

I watched helplessly as tears continued to flow down her cheeks. Both of us had seen horrendous atrocities that shouldn't be occurring in the modern world, but her experience had been fucking personal.

"What haunts you the most?" I asked insistently, wanting to help her kill off those ghosts.

She swiped the tears from her face and then turned her gorgeous turquoise eyes on me. There was a burning anger in her expression that would probably make the strongest person flinch, but I refused to back down.

"Can't we just let it go?" she snapped. "Because I really want to forget it, but I relive it over and over in my nightmares. I've been in counseling ever since it happened, and I still can't stop dreaming about it. I've dealt with the emotional trauma as much as I'm able to right now, but there are still times when I can't stop myself from remembering how I had wished they'd just kill me so I didn't have to endure another minute of pain or another minute of them using my body."

She was breathless by the time she'd finished, and I stared angrily at her tiny, vulnerable figure, and troubled eyes. I wasn't pissed at her for what she'd said. Dani had every right to hate talking about her experience. I was enraged by the unfairness of what she'd endured.

Dammit! Maybe I *had* once said she'd known the risks of her job. But that didn't mean I'd ever *wanted* her to suffer. "I'm sorry," I said in a husky voice. "I didn't mean to bring up something that hurts to talk about."

"It doesn't hurt anymore," she answered. "It majorly pisses me off. I want to move on. But my fear paralyzes me sometimes. I think I'm over what happened, and it comes back in my damn dreams. I lost my skills and a job that I loved because I just can't seem to pretend it never happened."

"It will eventually fade, but I'm not sure you ever completely get over an experience like that," I informed her grimly.

"Obviously I haven't," she said in a tremulous voice. "Not entirely." *Christ!* I felt like I was experiencing her pain. My heart was racing, and I did all I could not to carry her away again, and put her in a place where she'd never be harmed again. There was an unfamiliar ache in my chest for everything she'd been through. I felt like I was having a damn heart attack.

I can't stand to ever see her hurting again.

"Give up on Becker," I insisted. "He'll bring you nothing but more pain."

Her angry gaze met my stubborn one. "I can't. I won't," she answered determinedly. "He's the only thing that keeps me grounded and busy right now."

Unexpectedly, my temper flared. "Dating a criminal is *not* helping you."

"You have no idea what I need right now. You come here with nothing but rumors about a man who appears to care about me.

Nobody has ever found any solid evidence that Greg committed *any* crimes."

Oh, I'd find evidence. It was just a matter of time. In the meantime, I didn't want Dani anywhere near the investigations. "He's on everybody's watch list. For God's sake, do you want to get tangled up in that?"

She stood. "If I have to, I will." She stormed to the door and opened it. "Now please leave. I've dealt with all I can handle today."

I was furious, but nothing I could say would help her right now. I hesitated as I reached the door. "Do you actually love him?"

"I never said I loved him, but I need him right now," she retorted.

The last thing I wanted to hear was that she thought she needed Becker. She didn't. But maybe she was confused. "I'm not letting him take you down with him," I growled as I stepped out the door.

She didn't answer.

The door slammed closed right behind me.

Chapter 6

Dani

"**M**arcus drives me crazy, Harper. I don't understand why he's even here," I confided to my sister on the phone the next day.

Harper was the only person who really understood how I felt. I'd finally broken down and told her everything about what had happened to me while I was in captivity, right after I'd resigned from my network.

"Maybe he's right, Dani. Maybe you shouldn't be mixed up in any of this. Maybe dating Gregory Becker isn't a good idea," she answered in a concerned tone.

I flopped onto the sofa in the condo. My sister was an architect, but she operated far outside of corporations. And her husband was a US Senator. So she'd probably never heard any of the rumors that I knew circulated in the world of big business. "You're starting to sound just like Marcus," I told her in a disgusted voice.

"Marcus has been in the business world since he became an adult. If he's heard that this guy is bad news, I'm sure he knows something. He certainly isn't the type to overexaggerate."

"I'm not going to stop seeing Greg," I informed her stubbornly. "Do you know why Marcus is here?"

"I don't," she admitted. "But Blake mentioned that Marcus has real estate all over the world, so I'm not surprised that he owns property there."

Honestly, I wasn't surprised, either. I just wished he'd go spend time somewhere else. I found his presence unnerving when I was trying to establish a relationship. Especially when he was dragging me away from my dates. "I'm hoping he leaves soon."

"Don't bet on that," Harper warned. "He's obviously trying to protect you, and from what Blake has told me, he can be pretty stubborn."

"Why would he even care?" I asked desperately. "I barely know him. He *did* save my life, but it's not like we've kept in touch."

Truthfully, Marcus had been supportive when I'd shared some of what had happened to me during our long flight from Turkey to the US. Granted, I hadn't shared every single detail, but what I had confessed to him had been difficult to share. But I'd poured enough of my heart out to him that I couldn't quite seem to look at him as just an acquaintance. That description didn't quite fit. He'd ended up staying with me until I was finally exhausted and fell asleep on the bed in his private jet. When I woke up, we'd been landing in DC. But then, I couldn't honestly say Marcus was a *friend*, either. We hadn't seen each other since we'd parted ways in Washington.

"He's protective of his family," Harper answered. "And you're family to him now. I'm married to his twin brother."

"That's kind of a stretch," I replied. "I'm the sister of his sister-in-law."

"Obviously, that's close enough for him to be concerned." Harper sighed before she continued. "Despite his rather irritating arrogance, he's a good man, Dani. He lost his father when he was little more than a boy, and Blake says he's always felt like it was *his* responsibility to pick up the mantle for his father. His childhood was pretty much lost. He and Blake started to grow apart after their father died.

Marcus went to college and then traveled most of the time. It's only recently that they've started to build their relationship again."

Even though I was angry at Marcus, I felt a twitch of pain in my heart for the young man who had lost his father way too early. I could see Marcus trying to fill the void in the family. And he was the only one who had continued his father's legacy in international business. "Are the two of them close again?" I asked curiously.

"It's better than it used to be. But Marcus still keeps to himself way too much. Even Blake isn't privy to what he's thinking most of the time."

"I hope Blake has a better sense of humor than Marcus," I commented. "I'm not sure I've ever seen Marcus crack a smile."

I hadn't seen a lot of my sister and Blake. We'd talked at Harper's wedding, but it had been chaotic with all of the family around. After they'd married, I'd gone back to traveling in Europe for my job. I hadn't been back to Rocky Springs since I'd left my network. I'd come directly to Miami.

"Come to think of it, I don't think I've ever seen Marcus smile, either," Harper observed. "And Blake has a wonderful sense of humor. I think he's taught me how to have fun again."

I sighed. I wished I could remember what it was like to laugh. Honestly, I'd been pretty damn glum for months. "I'm glad," I said sincerely.

Harper deserved to be happy. My sister did so much for other people. Since she had tons of money like every other Lawson, she didn't have to work for a living. But she spent most of her time building homeless shelters around the country to help make a difference in the world.

At one time, I thought I'd been making my own mark on the planet. I let the world know about the atrocities that were happening in other countries and at home—up close and personal. Most of the reporting was pretty brutal, and I did it to bring awareness of what was happening in places most people probably rarely thought about.

Once…that had been important to me, more critical than my own safety. But after my experience in Syria, I couldn't do my job the same way anymore, and I hated it.

"Are you okay?" Harper asked in a kind tone.

"As okay as I *can* be, seeing as I quit my job," I answered honestly.

"How's the therapy going?"

"It's good. I still have flashbacks and nightmares, but otherwise I'm okay. I think I just need time."

"I worry about you. I wish you'd come for a long visit here in Colorado. Come stay with me. I'll be home for a few months. The Senate is out of session."

Although we'd grown up close to the Colters, we didn't have a home there anymore. After my parents had been killed in a traffic accident, we'd sold our childhood home. None of the brothers, me, or Harper could stand the pain of staying in our old home. There were too many memories and reminders that we'd lost our parents way too soon.

"I'll get there as soon as I can," I answered noncommittally. Right now, I didn't want to make any promises. I wasn't sure what was going to happen with Greg. "You could always feel free to come visit the condo that we bought but you never see," I teased.

I had used Miami as my home base most of the time when I was actually in the States. Either that, or I'd crashed at Harper's place in California, a home that she'd now sold to live full-time with her husband in Rocky Springs.

"I've seen the Miami condo," Harper argued. "I just don't spend as much time there as you do."

"It would be a comfortable flight on your husband's private jet," I pointed out.

Harper sighed. "I'd love to come there, but I don't get as much time with Blake as I'd like, and he's home until the Senate is back in session. I kind of miss the ocean. When we were growing up, I never missed the water. But now the lack of water is the only thing I don't like about Colorado. What people consider lakes here are actually ponds."

I smiled because I knew exactly what she meant. "Well, the ocean is here waiting for you when you're ready."

"I'll get there eventually, especially if you're still there. I need to meet this boyfriend of yours."

"Greg isn't exactly my boyfriend," I denied. "Not at the moment, anyway."

"He's still seeing other people?" Harper asked, sounding confused.

Actually, I was pretty sure Greg was still *fucking* other people. He wasn't really the faithful type. "Yes."

"Are you?" Harper questioned.

I hesitated, wondering if being so damn attracted to her husband's twin brother would count as some kind of infidelity. "I'm not seeing anybody else."

"If he hasn't seen you for the treasure you are, then maybe he isn't good enough for you," Harper said thoughtfully. "Are you certain that Marcus isn't right about this guy?"

I rolled my eyes. "Marcus isn't right about everything, and he has no business getting involved in who I date, Harper. It's annoying."

"I think that maybe you like Marcus," she answered. "You spent a lot of time with him while you were recovering. You said he was nice to you."

"I *don't* like him," I insisted. "And he was nice to me then. But he cheats at playing chess," I grumbled.

Harper laughed out loud. "How do you cheat at chess? Oh my God, did he actually beat you?"

"I think he switched pieces around when I wasn't looking," I informed her, knowing I was fibbing. Marcus had won fair and square, but I was kind of a sore loser when it came to chess games.

"He *did* win!" Harper exclaimed, sounding delighted.

"Don't sound so happy about it."

"You need a man who will challenge you once in a while," she declared. "You're too intelligent to date an ignorant male."

"Speaking of perfect men, how is Blake?" I asked, needing to change the subject. I pretty much told Harper everything, but because Marcus was her brother-in-law, I didn't feel comfortable spilling my guts about how much Marcus confused me.

"He's amazing," Harper said with a happy sigh. "Sometimes it's hard to believe that he's back in my life, and I'm married to him."

"Believe it. I was your maid of honor. I saw it happen."

"I know. But it still seems surreal. I just wish you and our brothers could find the same kind of happiness. Mason has gotten so cynical, and I'm worried about Jett after what happened with Lisette."

"I'd still like to bitch slap her," I confessed. "How do you dump a guy you love just because he had an accident and has a few scars and a limp? The accident hasn't changed who he is inside."

"She didn't love him. I'm glad she's out of his life," Harper admitted. "Jett is too good for her. There was nothing he wouldn't do to make her happy, and she treated him like dirt."

"Have you heard from him?" I asked, wondering how my youngest brother was getting along. "I haven't heard from him for a few days."

"He had to have another minor operation. But I talked to him yesterday, and he sounds okay."

Harper and I caught up on the rest of the family, finally hanging up because we both had things to do.

I went to the kitchen to put my phone on *charge*. I'd just connected it when it began to ring.

I checked the caller ID, my heart beginning to speed up as I saw that Greg was the caller. A surge of adrenaline shot through my body, a familiar feeling because I experienced it every time I talked to or saw Gregory Becker.

I took a deep breath and let it out to calm down before I finally answered the phone.

Chapter 7

Marcus

I t hadn't been difficult to get tickets to the charity event being held
in Miami Beach at some fancy club I'd never been to before. All
I'd had to do was cough up the required money for a ticket, and
I gained my entrance into the exclusive gathering, the place where
Gregory Becker would come through the door momentarily with his
date. I wasn't interested in *him* at the moment. I was here because
Danica was apparently coming here with him tonight.

Obviously, she wasn't prepared to listen to my advice, so I was
going to have to be more assertive and clear about her staying away
from Becker.

*Goddammit! Why did she have to be so damn stubborn? What
hold did Becker have over her?* I refused to acknowledge that she
might actually *like* the asshole.

I looked around the ballroom, a venue that was rapidly filling up
with guests. I'd grabbed a table that gave me a perfect view of the
only entrance to the room, and I'd already tossed back more than
one glass of Scotch while I'd been waiting.

George had driven me here, and he'd be waiting for me whenever I left, which I hoped would be soon. The large space was air conditioned, but the humidity was ruthless, and my tuxedo was starting to become uncomfortable as the place started to get overcrowded with guests.

Yeah, I'd attended plenty of these events, but I wasn't usually attending because I was pissed at a hot redhead who wouldn't listen to my warnings. I generally had a reason to come to a formal affair. Otherwise, I just sent a check to my charities and they were perfectly happy.

My blood pressure rose as Becker finally strolled through the door, looking just as pretentious as he had the few times we'd met in the past. But my hypertension was being caused by the woman he was manhandling, his arms around Danica's waist like he fucking owned her.

If anybody owns her, it's me!

My random thought startled the hell out of me. I wasn't a possessive kind of guy, and I'd *never* wanted a woman all to myself. Sure, I had my share of liaisons with women. My sexual appetite had always been healthy. Well, it *had* been *before* I went and kissed an angel who made me feel all kinds of bizarre emotions I'd never experienced before.

Really, I didn't want to *own* her, right? That was just sick and twisted.

Maybe *own* wasn't a good word, because I had no desire to control her other than moving her away from danger. *Okay. Yeah. I didn't want another man touching her either.*

After watching Dani for a few more seconds, I decided I *was* definitely sick and twisted when it came to her. The desire to punch Becker out and drag Dani away from him was still as strong as it had been when they'd walked through the door. Maybe worse!

It didn't help as my eyes roamed over Dani's form. I knew her well enough to recognize that her appearance wasn't really her usual style. The black dress she was wearing was a formal, but it had a figure-hugging design, and the hem landed well above her knees.

Once again, she was wearing a ridiculously high pair of stiletto heels that were black, and I had to pull my mind out of the gutter as I wondered what kind of lingerie she was wearing under that cock teaser of a dress.

Her hair was in a sleek bob, the black dress enhancing the red of those bouncy strands. I had *no* idea what was up with the heavy makeup she was wearing. From what I'd observed, she didn't seem like the type to layer makeup onto her skin. She certainly didn't need it to be fuckable. Really, all she needed to do was breathe and my dick was hard. I was pretty sure any guy with a healthy sex drive would feel the same way.

I motioned for a waiter to bring me another Scotch. I desperately needed it now that I'd seen Dani with Becker.

I watched as the couple progressed around the room, Dani quietly staying by Becker's side, the expression on her face not quite what I'd expect from a woman who was excited to be with her date. Her smile was weak and unnatural, and her demeanor was submissive, something I knew damn well wasn't normal.

The event was crowded and she'd never noticed my presence, which was just what I'd wanted. I'd situated myself that way purposely. I could watch her, but she wasn't seeing me.

Over the last year, I'd become damn good at stalking her undetected, which was something I wasn't exactly proud of, but I'd accepted the fact that I couldn't lose the overwhelming desire to protect her. The tendency was much too strong— even for me—to stuff back down and ignore.

Eventually, they moved to the bar. Becker shoved some pink and fluffy drink at Dani, and he accepted what I assumed was some kind of gin from the bartender.

It seemed like Becker was doing all the talking, because she was just nodding obligingly back at him with the same false smile.

Finally, she put her drink on the bar and then headed off alone. It was the moment I'd waited for and I discreetly followed her.

Because I'd been watching women coming in and out of the restroom, I had to wait for the last female I'd seen go in to exit again before I entered.

Dani was drying her hands by the time I plowed through the door. She took a superficial look at me. But within a blink of an eye, her gaze snapped back to me again with astonishment. "Marcus? What in the hell are you doing here? And you *can't* be in *here*. It's the *ladies'* room."

I didn't care *where* we were. Everyone was out of the restroom, and I needed to talk to her. I crossed my arms as I leaned against the counter. She wasn't going anywhere. "There's nobody else in here. Why are you with him, Danica? I warned you about Becker. I'm not here for no reason. He's dangerous."

"And I remember telling you that I wasn't about to heed your warning, Marcus," she answered tightly.

She tried to duck around me after she dried her hands, but failed miserably.

I moved to block her exit. "What is it with you and Becker? Does he have some kind of control over you? Because I sure as hell don't believe you're enjoying yourself."

She shrugged. "He's hot. He's rich. Plenty of women want to be with him."

My calm resolve was beginning to waver. I pinned her against the granite vanity where the sinks were located, preventing her escape. "That's bullshit, Dani, and we both know it." I swiped my hand against her cheek. "How many layers of makeup are you wearing?"

"Greg likes me to wear it like this," she protested, pushing against my chest. "And it doesn't matter to me."

"What in the hell do you need from him that you aren't getting? What is he doing for you? You told me you weren't sleeping with him."

"I'm not. But maybe I *want* to be with him," she answered angrily. "What in the hell does it matter to you?"

My ability to think rationally was challenged, and I was so incensed at the idea that she might want to sleep with Becker that I threaded a hand through that sleek, sexy red hair and lowered my head, my mouth crashing down on hers.

I wasn't gentle with her, but I *could* be. Dammit! She belonged in my bed and not Becker's. *Never* Becker's! I'd give her whatever the hell she needed to get away from that asshole.

I *felt* the exact moment she gave in to the kiss, her body melting against mine and her arms twining around my neck.

Any sense of reason I had was gone as I lifted my head, my breath sawing in and out of my lungs like I'd just run a marathon. *Fuck!* I could *not* resist this woman for some unknown reason. I wanted to claim her as mine, but I sure as hell couldn't do it here.

My hands stroked down her back and landed on her shapely ass. I kissed the sensitive skin of her neck as I lifted her short skirt in a damn frenzy.

My cock was rock-hard as I realized she was wearing very little under her dress. Just a tiny pair of panties and a garter belt to hold up those sheer stockings.

Her breathless moan of pure desire almost made me come undone as my hand moved between her thighs, where my fingers met her silken heat below her barely there panties.

"Does he make you feel *this*, Danica?" I asked demandingly, watching her head fall back as I stroked through her wet folds and teased the tiny bundle of nerves that was practically begging to be touched.

"Marcus. Somebody could come in here," she said, panting.

The throaty, needy tone of her voice as she said my name made my cock throb painfully.

I ignored it. *This wasn't about me...*

However, she *was* right about being too exposed, so I quickly yanked her into one of the stalls and closed the door. The upscale bathroom cubicle provided full enclosure except for overhead. It offered more privacy, yet I'd still be able to hear if somebody entered.

Dani's back was against the wooden wall, her expression raw and confused.

I stroked her cheek. "Does that turn you on, Dani? The thought that you might get caught while you come?"

She was adventurous. I knew that. And I honestly didn't give a damn if she was screaming my name when somebody entered. Hell, I'd welcome anybody who would know that she was *mine*.

"No, that's crazy," she said tremulously.

"Is it?" I asked, my fingers on her pussy again.

Her head slammed back against the wood, but she didn't seem to notice. "Oh, God. Why are you doing this?"

"Because I want you as much as you want me, Danica. I don't want Becker touching you. I want it to be *me* who makes you come every damn time," I rasped against the side of her neck.

My touch was firm on her clit, but not enough to send her over the edge. I was enjoying watching her pleasure too much for this to be over quickly.

"Why? Why me?" Her voice was quivering with raw passion.

"I have no fucking idea, but I really don't care anymore," I answered in a graveled voice.

I watched as she sagged against the wall, totally lost in the need to find her climax, her hips pushing against my hand frantically.

Jesus! She was fucking gorgeous when her face was relaxed, her beautiful eyes filled with need.

At some other place, I'd taste her, feast on her, and then fuck her until she became completely undone. But I didn't lose track of exactly where we were and the limitations that presented.

Regardless of the way she talked, I was fairly certain that she hadn't been with anybody since I'd kissed her. I knew what she'd been through at the hands of the terrorists. And it was going to take a guy who understood what she needed. And that man was going to be *me*.

I heard the bathroom door open, and I put a finger over her lips. I stroked over her clit faster, adding the pressure she was craving.

"Yes," she whispered, aware that somebody had come into the restroom, but unable to hold everything back.

I put my mouth close to her ear and whispered in a husky tone, "Come for me, Dani."

Her eyes closed and she bit her bottom lip, desperately trying to be quiet.

I used that moment to thrust my finger into her slick sheath, almost groaning myself at how tight, wet, and inviting that channel was as I added a second finger and thrust into her while my thumb still teased her clit.

One hand was on her ass, stroking over her exposed butt cheeks because she was wearing some sexy thong panties.

"Marcus!" she whispered urgently. "I can't."

"Oh yes, you can," I told her in a hoarse, low tone.

Her head thrashed, and I felt her body begin to tremble, so very close to release.

When she opened her mouth and her body tightened, I slammed my lips down hard over hers, swallowing her scream as her orgasm tore through her body. My hand on her ass supported her as her legs appeared to give way. I lifted my mouth and kissed her temple, my hand reaching back to lower the toilet seat before I helped her sit down on top of it.

She was gasping for breath as I removed a clean handkerchief from the pocket of my tux, crouched down, and gently wiped the sweat from her face.

I'd heard the water running out at the sink, and the guest left the bathroom, leaving us alone again. At least for now.

"Are you okay?" I asked, concerned that I'd pushed her too hard.

She wasn't afraid of me anymore, nor was she frightened of her own sexuality. Knowing that she'd been aroused without thinking about what had happened to her at the hands of her captives told me just how far she'd come with therapy.

She shook her head and then took the handkerchief from my hand to pat down her neck and face. "I don't know what happened to me," she confessed, still looking shaken.

"You came," I offered helpfully.

"It doesn't happen for me like that."

"Maybe it's what you need, Dani. And you aren't going to get it from Becker," I grumbled.

She stood up suddenly, forcing me to straighten up along with her. "Oh, God," she said anxiously. "Greg. He's going to be so mad. I've been in here too long."

I grabbed her arms and shook her lightly. "You can't keep dancing to his tune, Danica," I rumbled, angry about her concerned response.

"I have to," she said in a desperate voice. "I need him to trust me."

"Fuck no, you don't," I said to her forcefully. "You don't need his sorry ass at all."

"You don't understand," she said in a pleading voice. "I have to go back."

"Not happening," I answered. "Not until I have some answers. Christ! I just got you off, Dani. And you want to run back to Becker?" I was about ready to lose it.

"I need to get back to the party," she answered, trying to claw her way out of the stall.

I let her go because I couldn't stand to see her so terrified. Not after what she'd been through.

She sprinted to the mirror and tried to quickly fix her makeup and hair.

Finally, I said, "Go. Go back to him. But I'll be watching. You don't love him. Hell, I don't think you even enjoy being with him." I'd seen the way she looked at Becker, and it certainly wasn't how she'd looked at me with desperate passion in her eyes, her expression begging me to make her come.

I slammed out of the restroom, more furious than I'd been when I'd first come in to find Dani. *Jesus!* The woman was going to give me a damn heart attack. I slid into my seat at the table, my dick still as hard as granite.

Dani exited a few minutes later, her eyes searching for and finding Becker not far beyond where I was sitting.

It took everything I had not to block her way as her sexy ass got closer and closer, but to my surprise, she stopped at my table. She was watching Becker, but his back was to both of us.

Without missing a beat, she swiped my Scotch from my table and downed it in two big gulps and then set it back down on the pristine white tablecloth.

"I hate pink, fluffy drinks," she mumbled and then moved on toward her date.

I smirked. I had to admire a woman who could knock back a good whiskey without flinching.

My eyes never leaving Dani, I signaled the waiter for a refill.

Chapter 8

Dani

Greg was angry.

I'd known it from the moment he'd given me "the look" after I got back from the restroom at the charity event.

I'd stayed away from him way too long, and once I'd returned to his side, I was distracted.

Okay, I was *way* distracted.

It hadn't been easy standing with my date when I knew the guy who had given me a mind-blowing orgasm only moments before was staring a hole in my back.

What in the hell had gotten into me in the restroom? I'd lost complete control of myself and wallowed in the pleasure that Marcus had given me.

My body had craved Marcus's touch so desperately that I hadn't even thought about my date. My senses had been battered, and all I'd been able to do was ride a wave of heat so staggering that I was pretty sure I'd come away a little more than singed.

I'd never quite recovered from that volatile orgasm, and now that Greg and I had returned to my condo, I knew he was going to vent some of his anger.

"What in the hell was tonight about?" Greg asked angrily as I closed the door of my condo behind us after we'd entered.

Well, that hadn't taken very long.

"Would you like a drink?" I asked politely as I moved by him and into the kitchen.

He followed me. "No, I don't want a goddamn drink. I want you to tell me why you were gone so long to the bathroom. How long does it take to piss? I felt like you were with somebody else tonight, because you sure as hell didn't hear a word I said to you."

I turned back to look at him, noticing that his eyes were sparking with anger. "I was there. What else do you want from me? I've never been fond of fancy fundraisers."

I always gave my money readily enough, but I preferred to do it in private. I didn't need public adoration for donating money to a good cause the way Greg seemed to crave it.

He grabbed my hair and jerked my head back. "I want everything you have," he said bitterly. "I don't want your mind somewhere else when I'm speaking to you."

"Greg, that hurts," I said firmly, trying to pull back.

"I don't give a shit if it hurts. I want it to hurt. Maybe you'll remember who you answer to and who you're with."

His venomous stare was starting to scare me, but I didn't want him to know.

"Let. Go. Of. Me." I tried not to let him see me sweat.

Thankfully, his painful grip on my hair finally released, but I wasn't expecting the powerful backhanded blow he let fly on my face.

My cheek felt like it exploded, and my head jerked to one side. Tears filled my eyes from the pain. He hadn't held back. He'd let go full force.

My hand flew to my face, as I took a step back. "Why did you do that?"

He sneered. "Because I can," he answered darkly. "I'm your god-damn master, Dani. Haven't you figured that out by now? I'm in charge of any woman I date."

"I wore what you wanted. I did what you wanted," I reminded him.

"But I didn't have your complete attention. Do I have it now?"

I looked at him and nodded because I didn't think I could handle another blow like the one I'd just taken.

"Good," he answered smugly. "I think it's time I fucked you. Past time. Be at my house next Friday night, and wear something sexy."

I swallowed hard and kept silent as he moved forward and stroked a hand down my injured cheek. "I didn't want to have to do that to you," he said in an eerily calm voice. "You made me do it. I can't lose control of anything, especially my women. I don't share, Dani. I'll never share."

I couldn't very well say that he didn't have to share. Truth was, all I'd thought about all night was Marcus.

His fingers pushed sadistically on my throbbing cheekbone. "That will leave my mark," he mused. "I like it. Your face will be black and blue by my hand."

Jesus! I was hoping that was enough. I'd suffered through worse beatings at the hands of the terrorists. Much worse. But it was so much harder dealing with abuse from somebody when I wasn't a captive.

I let out a silent breath of relief as he turned and walked toward the door. "Next Friday. Be there or I'll come and find you, and it won't be pleasant for you," he threatened.

"I'll be there. What time?"

He seemed to consider my question for a moment before he answered. "Eight o'clock. Be on time, and plan on spending the night. My girls aren't usually capable of leaving after I'm done with them. I like it rough. *Very* rough."

I inwardly cringed, but outwardly showed no reaction to his comment. I was pretty sure he handled his women in bed the same way he did out of the sack.

I slowly followed him to the door and then opened it for him. "I'll see you then," I muttered.

He shot me a look totally devoid of emotion. "Don't disappoint me. I hate being disappointed."

"I won't," I agreed meekly.

I'd known that Gregory Becker had a very hard edge when I'd decided to go out with him. None of what was happening should be surprising, but it was a sharp contrast to what had happened with Marcus.

He turned and walked out the door, and I closed it with a heavy sigh.

My first priority was to get into the kitchen and get a bag of ice for my face. It hurt like hell, and I wasn't used to taking beatings anymore. It could have been a lot worse, but the volatile impact of his hand colliding with my face was causing my cheek to throb.

I held the ice to my face and kicked out of the high heels that were killing my feet.

All I wanted was to scrub off the layers of makeup from my skin, lose the butt-hugging dress I had on, and get into a warm bath.

I didn't want to think about what Greg had said.

I wanted to remember what Marcus had done to my body, and how I'd responded. Yeah, I knew that I could never let something like that happen with Marcus again, but I'd felt more alive when I'd been locked in a bathroom stall than I had in a very long time.

"I don't understand him," I murmured to myself.

Marcus could have very easily fucked me up against a bathroom wall, but all he'd done was get me off. Hard! It was almost like he said—that it really did give him an enormous amount of pleasure just to see me come.

"What guy does that?" I asked myself.

There was only one answer: Marcus Colter.

I'd been so lost in the scent of him, the taste of him, the passion in his kiss, and the raw carnality of the moment that he could have satisfied himself very easily. But he hadn't.

The rest of the night had been uncomfortable, and my mind *hadn't* been on my date. Greg had needed to repeat himself several times, and my mind *had* wandered from the superficial conversations he was having with the other guests.

I'd been able to *feel* Marcus watching me, even when my back was to him. He'd still been at the same table he'd been sitting at all night when Greg and I had left the event.

Just as I was headed toward my coveted bathtub to get water ready, my doorbell rang. My heart raced at the thought that Greg had come back for another round of abuse.

I dropped my ice pack on the side table next to the couch.

After moving close to the door, I opened it cautiously, braced for whatever Greg was going to throw at me this time.

"Marcus," I said in a breathless voice. My body sagged in relief, happy I wasn't going to have to face Greg again.

I let him in and closed the door quickly behind him, noticing he was still wearing his tux.

"Are you okay?" he questioned in a husky voice.

"Yeah, I'm fine," I replied. "What are you doing here?"

"I need to talk to you," he told me urgently. "Dani, somehow I need to make you understand that you don't need Becker. I don't want to see you hurt."

The gruff, concerned tone of his voice nearly broke me. I looked at him pleadingly. "Please, Marcus, not now."

I wasn't capable of any further conflict. I still struggled with some issues from my kidnapping, and I was shaken by Greg's treatment just a short time earlier.

"What in the hell happened to you?" he asked in a terrifyingly angry voice.

I stepped back from him, but he proceeded forward, wrapping his arm around my waist while he tipped my face up. "Dani, did that bastard hit you?" His fingers trailed, featherlight, over my cheek.

"It's no big deal. I made him mad." I tried to pull away, not because his touch hurt me, but because Marcus affected me in ways I didn't understand.

"I'll fucking kill him," he growled, his gray eyes swirling with fury. "What the fuck! Why are you letting this happen, Danica? Make me understand, and *then* I'll go after the little prick."

I could feel the tension in his body, and his willingness to sprint back out the door to track down Greg. "Marcus, no. You can't confront him right now."

"Oh, yes, I damn well can, and I will. Only a damn coward wales on a woman half his size," he ranted. "And who gives a fuck if he got mad? That's no excuse. There's never an excuse for touching a woman with the intent of hurting her in any goddamn way. I get mad. *My* brothers get mad. *Your* brothers get mad. My friends get mad. What they *don't* do is punch a woman in the face."

"He didn't punch me. He backhanded me."

"Just the fact that he touched you at all is a good reason for me to hunt him down. He can't hurt you like this, Dani. Christ! Does he know what you've been through? Does he even care?"

"No," I said softly. "No to everything. He doesn't really know me at all."

A sob escaped my mouth. Then another. And then one more. Tears started to flow free in a river down my face. "Don't leave me right now. Don't go to find him," I pleaded.

"Give me one good reason why I shouldn't," he grumbled.

He was hesitating, his hand running up and down my back in comforting strokes.

"Because I need you more," I said in a helpless tone, flinging my arms around his neck, knowing I had to let go and share my secrets.

Chapter 9

Dani

Mindlessly sobbing my heart out wasn't something I was used to doing, but it seemed so easy to just let it happen when Marcus was holding me against him, his solid body making me feel safe.

He lifted my body easily and then sat down on the couch, holding me on his lap while I released all of my sorrow, frustration, and fear.

He didn't ask any questions.

He didn't try to make me stop crying.

All he did was hold me, comfort me, giving me something I'd never had before.

"I hate crying," I finally admitted with a hiccup.

His mouth by my ear, he said in a teasing voice, "For something you hate, you seem to be doing a lot of it."

I smiled just a little, thinking that it was a typical *Marcus* kind of comment. But there was a thread of kindness running through the teasing tone, and that made me feel protected.

Honestly, Marcus made me feel safe to be myself, and I really needed to feel that way right now. "I think I'm done now."

"By all means, feel free to continue," he answered drily. "Having your shapely ass draped over my dick doesn't bother me at all."

"You're completely perverted," I accused as I gingerly swiped at my eyes.

"No, Dani. I'm worried about you."

Those four simple words made my heart ache. I was used to traveling around, taking care of myself. I was alone. Always alone. I'd had a relationship in college, and I'd tried to have some kind of connection with a male correspondent, but it hadn't ended well. Both of us traveled so much that we rarely got to meet up, and it had felt more like a friends-with-benefits type of thing. We finally broke it off, and I'd never even tried again. What was the point? I was always in motion, and no relationship had a chance when I traveled that much.

Most of the time, I didn't mind relying on myself. I was used to going solo. But since Harper had found Blake, and after being held captive by a ruthless group of rebels, I recognized the emptiness in my soul. Problem was, I couldn't just fill it by being with somebody. Many times, I'd be in a crowded room, but I still felt like I was alone. I'd never realized how much I craved that one person who would make me feel like I wasn't lonely. Life experiences had changed me, and I couldn't seem to completely fall back to the way I'd been before my kidnapping.

I guess my priorities had changed along with my personality.

"You don't have to worry about me," I argued.

I knew I could move now that I'd stopped crying, but the scent and feel of Marcus just felt so good that I didn't even try.

His arms tightened around me. "For fuck's sake, Dani, you're dating a sociopath who just backhanded you until your face was black and blue." He stroked a hand through my hair before adding, "Which reminds me, we need to treat that cheek."

"I have ice," I informed him, reaching over to the side table for the cold pack.

"Let me have it," he rumbled, gently resting the pack on my face before he slowly slid me onto the couch so he could get up.

"Where are you going?" I hated that my voice sounded slightly panicked.

"You need to take something for pain and inflammation. Do you have that here?"

I had moved my hand to keep the cold pack on my face, and as I moved to get up, he protested. "Stay there," he demanded. "I'll find it."

I tried not to notice that Marcus's gruff protectiveness was one of the best things I'd experienced since my kidnapping. Maybe I shouldn't find it as sweet as I did. It wasn't like he was pouring on the charm because he really wasn't all that charming. Or maybe he wasn't to most people. But I found him nearly irresistible. Meaningless words and actions weren't Marcus's style, which made his protective instincts heartbreakingly adorable.

I directed him to the kitchen cupboard. I wasn't able to see his face once he opened the door, but I could hear him rifling through the items impatiently until he found what he wanted.

He brought some ibuprofen and a glass of ice water.

"Nobody has taken care of me for a long time," I mentioned as I accepted the items from him, dutifully swallowing the pills.

"I'm starting to think you need a damn bodyguard," he said in a disgruntled tone as he sat back down on the sofa next to me, and took over holding the cold pack to my face and gathered me into his arms.

I sighed as I curled my feet beneath me and leaned against him. "Are you applying for the job?"

"Hell, no. I'd probably kill any guy who got within ten feet of you. I can't watch this, Danica. I can't see somebody hurt you again," he answered in a husky, annoyed tone. "It nearly killed me to see what the rebels had done to you, and I can't get the images of them abusing you out of my damn head. I know you made a mistake by crossing the border, but you did it to save some stupid teenagers. I get that. But why in the hell would you let *Becker* do this to you? Why?"

I took a deep breath and let it out slowly before I answered. "It took me some time to get my head straight after we came back to the US.

I had intensive therapy, but I was suffering from PTSD and anxiety. It was so bad I was afraid of almost everything and everyone at first."

"Understandable," Marcus remarked. "Anybody would have felt the same way."

"But I hated it. I've never been afraid of anything. I traveled the world alone."

"You're definitely fearless," he agreed.

"No, I *was* fearless, Marcus," I said. "Now I have to push through the fear I never felt before. I've come a long way in counseling, and after I'd become a little more stable, I remembered something I'd heard while I was in captivity. I remembered after I'd gotten over the initial trauma."

"What?"

"I told you that I speak and understand Arabic, right?"

"Yeah."

"The terrorists mentioned Gregory Becker's name. Marcus, he's helping to fund the rebels. He's laundering funds to them. And I mean *a lot* of money. They consider him their leader in their war to take over territory because he's the money behind it. His disgusting businesses like human trafficking and drugs help get the rebels to take more and more areas."

He didn't question my knowledge. "Jesus Christ! Why? I heard he was funding terrorists, but I never understood it. What in the hell does he have to gain?" he rasped.

"Money and power," I told him. "He thinks the rebels are going to take control, which will give *him* control of the oil and resources. He doesn't give a damn what their motivation might be. All he wants is to be king of the resources that will make him the richest man on earth. It's crazy, but that's the way he thinks."

"Then why are you with him, Dani? If you overheard all this, what are you doing here? Why would you want to be with an asshole like him?"

I sighed, knowing it was time for me to be straight with Marcus. "I couldn't go back to my Middle East beat, so I decided to get an exclusive story right here in my own country. He needs to be stopped.

And nobody can get the evidence to convict him. I've heard he keeps a record of his illegal transactions so he knows how much money has been funneled to the terrorists, and by what method or shell company. If I can find that journal, I'd have the information to have him put away forever. The funding to the terrorists would stop, and he wouldn't be able to keep luring women into prostitution or human trafficking."

"Fuck! You were planning on exposing him yourself?" Marcus exploded.

"Not exactly. I was going to take the information to the authorities, and time my exclusive to come out the same day they arrest him. Obviously, they'd need time to track down the evidence in a more substantial form than just a journal. But those records would give them the information they need to do it."

"So you don't love Becker?"

I tried to shake my head against his shoulder. "No."

"Why did you say you needed him?"

"I *do* need him. I have to gain his trust. He finally asked me to come to his house, so I can get access to his home office and get what I need."

"You don't like being with him?"

"I like being with him as much as I'd like being in a locked room with venomous snakes," I said with a shudder. "I can barely stand next to him. I can't stand it when he touches me, and I have to hold back my hatred while he's kissing me."

"The bastard kissed you?" Marcus asked in a pissed-off tone.

"What choice did I have but to pretend I was hot for him? But every moment of it has been pure torture. However, if I can help take him down, it will be worth it."

"The clothes?"

"He chooses exactly how he wants me to look. Becker is a control freak. Unfortunately, he's fond of the hooker attire. He's an asshole who thinks he owns every female he dates or screws. There isn't an ounce of decency in him, Marcus, and believe me, I've looked. He's pure evil."

It felt good to finally tell somebody why I was trying to get close to Becker, but I knew it was going to cause complications.

"I'm relieved you haven't lost your common sense completely, and you see Becker for what he is, but you can't do this alone. And you can't see him again, Danica. The abuse will just get worse from now on, and you're putting your ass in danger...*again.*"

"I'm not quitting. I've already gotten close to him, close enough to get the information we need to put him away."

I'd known I had to tell Marcus the truth. He deserved it. He'd saved my life, and I really didn't want him to continue to think I was submitting to a crazed lunatic. I was hoping if I told him the truth, he'd stop riding my butt about not seeing Becker again. Apparently...not.

"You're quitting. If I have to, I'll kidnap you myself," he said in a demanding voice.

I sat up and stared him in the eyes. "Try it. I'm not budging. Too many other people's lives are at stake. Greg has to be stopped. He's power hungry, and things could get even worse than they are now. What if he decides he needs to win more territory, more wars? He's a master at covering his ass. He's wary, paranoid, and devious as hell. Obviously he's been a suspect for a long time, but nobody has been able to take him down. The authorities need information, data I can give them if I can just get to it."

"So you're just going to go to his home, fuck him, then look for the information?"

I shook my head slowly. "I don't think I can let him touch me like that. I think I'll throw up. I have to think of another way."

"You make me crazy, woman. First, I'm rescuing you from the hands of people who would have eventually killed you, and now you're getting yourself in too deep at home. This is risky and dangerous."

"I can handle this, Marcus. I know I can. I have to do it to prove that I can still do something important. When I wasn't able to go back to the Middle East, I missed it. There, I felt like I was telling important stories. I wanted people to understand the human suffering that was happening in that region. What I did meant something back then, and even though it might have been somewhat risky, bringing information out of those areas was vital. I lost that. Now I want to do something that's going to help people again. I want to be done with being afraid. I want to do something useful."

"You're not doing this alone," he insisted as he pulled my body against him again. "I can't see you taking those kinds of risks."

"I have no choice. Until I get the information, nobody will be able to touch him." I sighed. "I have a friend I made here in Miami, a woman who was homeless and was taken in by what I believe is one of Greg's human trafficking teams. They lured her in with a story about helping her get on her feet with a job, shelter, and food. Now they're telling her that she owes them, and that she can't leave until she pays them back. These jerks prey on the most vulnerable of people. Ruby was young. She hasn't even hit her twenty-third birthday yet, and they want to auction her off so some rich man can use her body. This makes it even more personal to me. And the worst part is that I can't take her in. I can't help her and break my trust with Greg right now. But something has to happen soon. I have to rescue Ruby, and all the money is going to do is make the rebels stronger."

"Jesus! You're so damn stubborn. Why can't you understand that I will *never* let you do this alone? I get why you want to do it, but it's a risk you can't take by yourself. And you can't meet Becker again. If I see as much as a tiny scratch on you, I'll lose it."

"I'll fight him. I won't hold back and let him hurt me again. I can't. It's not good for my psyche."

"That's not enough. I'm going to help you, Dani, and it's going to be on my terms."

I was alarmed. "Marcus, you can't. It's dangerous enough for me, but for a man who is on his tail, it's suicidal. He'd kill anyone who he thought was trying to dig up dirt on him."

"He won't suspect me," he said nonchalantly.

"What makes you think that?"

"Because there are things you don't know about me either, Dani, things nobody knows except my family."

"What?" I asked breathlessly because his voice had suddenly turned so grim.

"I have the knowledge and the expertise to help you nail Becker."

"How?"

"Because I've been gathering intel for a very long time. I'm not *just* an international businessman."

I was silent, waiting for his explanation.

He continued matter-of-factly, "I'm also a spy."

Chapter 10

Dani

A spy?

Lord help me, I'd never thought of Marcus as delusional, but what he'd just uttered made no sense.

"What do you mean?" I asked hesitantly.

He answered calmly. "I mean that I work with the US government to gather intel from all of the countries I visit. I have a network of contacts, and I get whatever information I can to protect our national security."

"Intel is CIA stuff," I answered, still wondering where he was going with this conversation.

"Technically, I'm not on the CIA payroll. I'm a special agent because I chose to be."

My mind flashed back to every location where I'd seen Marcus in the past. It had occurred to me so many times that he didn't need to put himself in harm's way, but he was in every hot spot in the world.

Sweet Jesus! Could what he was saying really be true? "H-how?" I stammered, still unable to reconcile Marcus the businessman with

Marcus as some kind of James Bond. Not that the CIA really worked like the movie portrayals, but still...

He shrugged. "It's not a big deal. I mostly just gather intelligence, and I've never really been suspect because I travel the world for business."

"Marcus, you do it in foreign countries where you could be killed by anybody who finds out you're sharing their information," I said, astonished that a man as rich as Marcus would put his butt on the line like that.

"I don't generally broadcast what I'm doing," he answered drily.

"It's dangerous," I protested. "Who do you have for backup?"

"No one. I answer only to the top government officials. Nobody else knows."

"What does your family think about these extracurricular activities? Have you told them that you're going all James Bond while you're traveling overseas?"

He released a masculine sigh. "First of all, special agents *don't* go James Bond. Sometimes it's actually rather boring."

"Do you carry a gun?" I challenged.

"Of course. But a lot of people do."

"Marcus, don't bullshit me. Poking around in some third world countries could get you murdered."

"Being a foreign correspondent can be just as bad. If I remember correctly, I *did* pull your gorgeous ass out of a rather ugly situation."

He had me there. My job had put me too close to the front lines at times. "I was doing it for a cause. People need to know what's happening in the world."

"And I do what I do for my country. I hate politics, and I don't like being involved in DC bullshit. That's why my help is kept low profile. I wouldn't last ten minutes doing Blake's job as a senator. Right now, country doesn't come before party for most of the DC crowd. It's all about money. I'd put my fist in somebody's face if I had to spend very long in Washington."

I tried not to smile because we were talking about something dead serious, but I could see Marcus losing his patience in one hell of a hurry on the hill. He didn't have the personality for that scene.

"You never answered my question about your family. Have they always known? How long have you been an agent?" I questioned, wanting to know everything at once. Honestly, I was still dumbstruck from his revelations. It wasn't that I didn't think Marcus had the balls for that kind of work, but it was a part of him I'd never seen before, and I was fascinated.

"They didn't know until recently. I had to tell them when one of my investigations got a little too close to home."

I listened closely as he told me about how his brother, Tate, and a female FBI agent had gotten inadvertently involved in an arms smuggling deal.

"So Tate ended up married to the FBI agent?" I queried when he was done with his story. I hadn't been back to Colorado in years, so I had no idea what the Colters were doing. Jett occasionally talked about Marcus, but other than a brief mention of the family by my brother, I was in the dark.

"Yeah. I was glad he met Lara. She's good for him, but I've never forgiven myself for nearly getting both of them killed. From that moment on, I never did anything that could even remotely endanger anyone in my family. If I can't deal with the situation completely out of the country, I don't get involved. I felt like I owed it to my family to let them know what I was doing."

"Don't they worry?"

"All the fucking time," he answered in a disgruntled voice. "My mother is terrified somebody will kill me every time I leave."

"Can you blame her? She loves you."

"Tate was Special Forces. That was a hell of a lot more dangerous than what I do."

"Had I known what you and Jett were doing with PRO, I would have been anxious every time you left," I told him honestly.

My brother had kept his involvement with PRO a secret until the mission where he was injured and the group shut down. Had I known they were sneaking into dangerous territory to rescue political prisoners, I know both Harper and I would have been worried sick.

Now, Marcus's forming of PRO in the first place made sense. He'd obviously learned his covert operation skills from years of spying on other countries.

"We saved lives," he stated. "But I doubt I'll ever stop feeling guilty about Jett's injuries. He's the only one who will probably never fully recover. He'll always carry the scars."

I saw the tension in his expression and reached out to smooth out the lines on his face. "Don't. You can't change what's already done. It was an accident. He's alive. It was nobody's fault, Marcus. You *did* save lives, and Jett told me he'd do it all over again."

He caught my hand in his and lowered our conjoined hands to his thigh. "He told me the same thing several times. But he lost everything that meant something to him."

"He lost *Lisette,* and it was the best thing that could happen. She didn't love him. He would have ended up miserable."

"Yeah. And I hear she's in trouble anyway. Something about some kind of tax fraud," he mentioned casually.

I shot him a curious look. "Tax fraud? How would you know that? Do you know her?"

"Nope. Never met her. But I do have a friend at the IRS. Seems she's been a little less than honest about paying her taxes."

"You got her in trouble?" I asked incredulously.

"Absolutely not. She's the one who didn't pay her taxes. It must be tough now that she's cut off from Jett's money."

It struck me as funny that Marcus could share that information without ever tipping his hand. If I didn't know he'd instigated the investigation on Lisette, I'd swear he was completely innocent. "You're bad," I told him, secretly happy that the woman who had dumped my brother so heartlessly was now in a mess of trouble. "Honestly, I'm glad she's paying in some way for what she did to Jett."

"Oh, she's going to be paying," Marcus remarked casually.

Just the fact that he'd tried to avenge Jett was pretty damn awesome. I'd never seen that side of Marcus. Really, I hadn't ever known him at all. His arrogance annoyed me at times, but if he was spying on foreign countries, he had to have balls of steel. "Thank you," I said softly.

"Jett is my friend," he stated simply. "And now we need to stop talking about me and get back to this issue with Becker."

"I can't give up, Marcus. And it isn't all about a scoop. Becker has to be stopped for many reasons." People like Ruby and everyone Greg was putting in danger needed somebody to fight for them. If I could help put him away, I was going to do it.

"He's been on our radar for a long time. But without solid evidence, there isn't much we can do. He's a slippery bastard," Marcus grumbled.

"He's paranoid," I agreed. "He's anal about covering all his bases."

"What's your plan?" he asked unhappily.

"I'm going to have access to his house next Friday. He wants me to meet him there in the evening. Somehow I have to get into his home office. I think that's where he keeps his records of his nonbusiness transactions. If I can get those, they can be tracked and confirmed pretty quickly."

Marcus took the ice pack I'd let slide away from my face and held it gently back on my cheek. "This is all crazy. You know that, right? Becker is an international criminal and has never hesitated to eliminate anybody who gets in his way."

I nodded. "I learned that the hard way."

"Christ! I hate this, Dani. I hate you getting involved with him. I hate the fact that you put yourself in danger. I hate that the fucker actually hit you, and I can't kill him for that. Just the fact that he's touched you in any way makes me insane," he finished with a growl.

My heart was pounding against my chest wall, the intense look on Marcus's face reminding me of our earlier encounter. "Then help me," I pleaded, knowing I could use his expertise. I was in over my head, and I was smart enough to know it. I didn't want to get him involved, but I knew it was the only way he wouldn't sabotage my efforts.

"I'm going to do more than help you. I'm going to be your partner. And if you do a single thing that I don't agree with, you're out of there," he demanded.

"Okay," I murmured, willing to agree to his terms. I had no doubt he could execute a plan better than I could.

"You should still be recovering, not putting yourself into another bad situation," he muttered irritably.

I gave him a weak smile. "I guess I've never been good at being idle."

"I'll make sure you don't get hurt, and then I'll insist on you taking some downtime. It hasn't been that long since you nearly died, Danica. You *need* to take some time off, whether you want to or not. You can find something a hell of a lot less dangerous to do."

Not staying busy did nothing but remind me how much I'd isolated myself. Before, I'd spent so much time chasing stories that I never really thought about how alone I felt. Sure, I had great siblings, but they were all busy with their own lives. "Time off gets lonely," I admitted before I could stop myself.

Marcus's arm snaked around my waist, and he pulled me against his very solid, warm body. "You're not alone anymore, Dani," he stated in a husky voice.

I absorbed his warmth, soaking it up like a sponge. Honestly, maybe the reason Marcus and I had fought so much in the past was because we were both so much alike in some ways. We were both independent, and we'd spent our whole adult lives traveling by ourselves. Neither of us had ever had somebody to lean on or talk to about how we felt. Both of us had put emotion aside like it wasn't important.

The problem was, I couldn't ignore how I was feeling anymore.

I laid my head against his shoulder and breathed in his masculine scent, feeling like I *wasn't* really alone. At least for a little while.

Chapter 11

Marcus

"Hey man, what's happening with my little sister?" Jett Lawson asked as I opened the door of my condo the next afternoon.

I was surprised, but I probably shouldn't be. Nothing kept Jett down for very long. "I thought you were having surgery," I answered, slapping him on the back as he entered with a canvas bag slung over his shoulder.

"They did it yesterday. It was no big deal," he answered, dropping his bag on the floor. "How do you feel about having a visitor? I wanted to see if I could talk some sense into Dani."

"You don't ever need to ask if you can stay with me. You always have an open invitation." I was glad to see him, but I felt a little bit guilty over the fact that I was lusting after his sister, and it kept getting worse every single day.

He dropped his bag on the floor. "Thanks. So what's up with Dani?"

I moved into the living room to get us a drink. Jett followed behind me with a slight limp. He was doing okay, but his leg bothered him when he did too much, which was pretty much all the time. My friend had a tenacity that humbled me sometimes. I knew he'd come out of his accident with injuries that not many people could survive, but he kept himself in optimal condition, which had probably saved his life. He was stubborn, but it was a quality that served him well right now.

"There's a lot happening that you don't know about," I warned him as I went to the bar to pour us a drink.

Jett flopped onto the couch. "Good or bad?"

I grimaced. "Both. The good news is that your sister isn't in love with an asshole. The bad news is that she's gotten herself into a situation that's going to be messy."

I caught him up with the whole situation with Becker, and then answered his questions after I'd handed him a drink and took a seat in the chair next to the sofa.

Jett shook his head. "I love my sister, but sometimes I wish she'd take up something a little less adventurous to do for a living."

"It's not just about a story for her anymore, Jett."

"Shit! I know that," he replied with frustration. "But I feel so damn helpless to do anything to help her."

"I'm helping her," I reassured him. "One sign of danger and I'm pulling her out."

"And she agreed?" Jett questioned skeptically.

I shrugged. "More or less. Probably less than more, but her ass is gone if Becker so much as looks at her the wrong way."

"Knowing that he hit her makes me want to kill the bastard," Jett said irritably.

I knew exactly how he felt. Dani had been through so damn much, and until last night, I'd never seen her really lose it. She was so damn brave, but her courage made me nervous as hell. Maybe she'd become a bit warier after her kidnapping, but her sense of justice and duty was still just as strong as it had always been. "We can't kill him," I finally answered unhappily. "We have to find out who else is involved."

J. A. Scott

"You have a good system here? I could try to do some checking," he offered. "I think if we knock out the kingpin, the rest will fall. But it wouldn't hurt to try to do some digging for information."

I shot him a knowing look. "You mean some *hacking*?"

"Hell, no. That would be completely illegal," he said in feigned protest.

I smirked at him, knowing that Jett had no problem hacking into a system if he needed vital information. He'd done it plenty of times for PRO missions, and he was one of the best at it. "I have everything set up in my office. Feel free to search for information. But before you get started, there's something I need to tell you."

Since I'd come clean with Danica, I needed to do the same with Jett. I wanted him to have confidence that I could help his sister, and telling him about my history would probably help. Hell, Jett was like a brother to me, so it would be like telling family. I'd trust him with my life, so I could tell him my secrets, too.

I informed him about my dual careers as briefly as possible.

"Holy shit, man," Jett said. "So you go all James Bond in foreign countries."

I shot him a disgusted look and then rolled my eyes. "You of all people have to know that nobody does *James Bond*. They're movies. Fictional characters. I'm pretty sure most agents sit behind a desk most of the day and try to dig up computer intel." I hesitated before adding, "Maybe you should be a special agent instead of me. I think they need your skills more than mine."

"Don't downplay what you're doing, buddy," Jett said in a serious tone. "It's dangerous, and it's pretty damn patriotic to risk your ass to keep our country safe."

"It's not a big deal. I have to travel anyway."

"But you don't *have* to spy for intel. That could get you killed. I don't know a lot of rich guys who'd do the same."

"You'd do it," I challenged.

Jett shrugged. "Maybe. We're both crazy adrenaline junkies. Maybe that's why we're such good friends."

"Just like your sister," I accused. "She's just as nuts as we are. Not a good quality for a woman who has already been through hell."

"She's always been that way," Jett commented thoughtfully. "Even when we were kids, she was pretty fearless."

I could hardly tell Jett that I hated her courage right now. Dani made me half crazy, and I needed to get a grip on my irritation. Jett's sister was off-limits. I wanted to fuck her worse than I've ever wanted any woman. But I also admired her, and the last thing I wanted was friction with my best friend because I was having a fling with his little sister. Dani and I could never have anything more than a brief affair. I wasn't capable of having a relationship. I never had been. I traveled too much, and I had very little to offer a woman except money.

"I don't like this," I admitted. "I don't like any of it. Becker is a prick. Your sister could find herself tangled up in something she can't handle."

"I don't like it, either," Jett confessed. "I'd get her away from here now if I could, but you know how stubborn she can be when she has her mind made up to do something. All of us tried to talk her out of her chosen career, especially being a Middle East correspondent. Not a single one of us could make her budge. She loved her job, Marcus. Dani is the type of woman who wanted to expose everything that's wrong with the world and drag it out into the open."

"I fucking know that. It's part of what makes me crazy. She has good intentions, but she puts herself in too much danger."

"Hey. You sound really concerned. You okay?" Jett asked.

I knew what he meant. I was generally a prick, and pretty free from emotional entanglement. But there was something about Danica that made me want to protect her. I could tell myself it was because of her past experience of being at the mercy of madmen, but to be honest, the compulsion had *always* been there. It was just getting harder and harder to ignore.

Somehow, in some insane way, we *got* each other. I understood her, and strangely enough, she seemed to have gotten under my skin. There was some force pushing us together, and I felt almost helpless to stop the stream of unfamiliar feelings that rose up every time I saw her.

But my emotional involvement had to stop. I needed to think like a professional, help her in any way I could, and stop worrying about her so damn much.

"Yeah," I finally replied. "I'm good."

"Is something going on between you and Dani?" Jett asked suspiciously.

"Not at all," I answered smoothly.

Nothing except a certain encounter where I got your sister off in a public bathroom just so I could watch her come.

But I wasn't about to go there with Jett.

"She's an amazing woman," he pushed. "It wouldn't be that surprising if you *were* attracted to her. Actually, you two are a lot alike."

"I'm not attracted to her," I denied. "I like her and she's your sister. I want to help her."

Jett looked like he wanted to say more, but he dropped the subject. "If Becker is as paranoid as Dani says he is, I doubt she's going to be able to get the documents you need out of his house."

"I've thought about that," I informed him. "I'm going to get some special equipment from the department."

"Spy gadgets?" Jett asked jokingly.

"Actually, yeah. Sometimes being an agent comes in handy. They have technology that most people don't."

Jett polished off his drink and then stood up. "You know I'm going to want to see them."

"I know," I answered elusively.

"I'm going to go try out your system. See what I can find out on Becker."

"Just don't do anything illegal on my computers," I warned, knowing damn well that Jett was so good at what he did that he'd never get caught.

"No promises," Jett mumbled. "If my sister's life is at stake, I'll do what I have to do. I may not have much as far as physical capabilities, but I do have skills."

"I'm well aware of that," I told him. I knew that he was one of the best when it came to computer spying, information gathering, and anything else on the web or the dark web.

"Takeout for dinner? Pizza would be good. I'm starving."

"I don't generally do pizza. Hell, I've never figured out how you eat so much junk food and still manage to stay in shape." Jett had always been physically strong, and even though he was injured, he was still pretty bulked up.

"I work out," he said defensively. "And I don't always do junk food."

"Only ninety-nine percent of the time," I said in a sarcastic tone.

He grinned. "Then you admit that I occasionally eat healthy?"

"Hardly ever."

"Like you should talk," Jett joked. "Half the time you eat on the run and do protein drinks. We could both use some protein *and* carbs right now."

"Fine. I'll order pizza," I conceded.

It wasn't that I didn't *like* pizza, burgers, fries, and all of the other things guaranteed to give me early heart failure, but I tried to avoid them, and I worked out as often as possible. I was in my mid-thirties, and I wasn't getting any younger. With all the traveling and CIA business I had to do, I needed to be able to keep my body in the best shape possible.

"I want it loaded," he insisted as he walked toward my office.

"As much grease as possible?" I asked.

"You got it," he answered with a laugh as he disappeared through the door leading to my sophisticated computer system.

My stomach growled, and I realized that I was hungry, too. Usually I'd send George out to find me a healthy meal. Instead, I found myself looking up pizza joints and calling in a very large order.

Dani

"Touch that last piece of pizza and you're a dead man," I warned my brother, Jett, as I snatched the last slice of the heavily loaded pie and slapped his hand away.

Generally, I wasn't the type to invite myself over to somebody's house, but when I heard that my brother was in town, I'd hightailed it over to Marcus's place. Luckily, I'd arrived just as the pizza was delivered.

I had impeccable timing when it came to food.

"I'm certainly not going to fight you for it," Marcus commented drily.

I chewed and swallowed a heavenly bite of the greasy pizza before I answered, "You didn't eat much."

"He's a food snob," Jett informed me. "He doesn't like junk food."

"I didn't say I don't like it," Marcus argued. "It's just not healthy."

We were all sitting around the dining room table at Marcus's condo. Of course, I made sure I was closest to the food. "What *is* healthy anymore?" I asked.

"Certainly not a ton of grease and cardboard," Marcus answered stuffily.

I couldn't argue with the fact that the man was in prime condition. But he was way too regimented. "So no chocolate?" I asked.

"Rarely," he confirmed.

"And I suppose you don't eat food from street vendors?"

"Never."

Good Lord, he really needed to lighten up. Yeah, I probably ate way too much fast food or things that I got on the go. I was usually too impatient to cook, and being on the road all the time made it difficult to grab anything except fast food.

"How do you eat when you're traveling?"

Marcus shrugged. "I usually have one of my assistants find me something decent."

"So where are your assistants now?"

He shot me a disgruntled expression as he answered, "I didn't have time to get somebody to meet me here, and it was personal. I had to chase down some crazy female. And since it wasn't business, I came alone."

I kind of liked the fact that Marcus had done something spontaneous and specifically because he was concerned about me, even though he *had* just called me *crazy*.

"So none of them know about your assistance to the government?" Jett chimed in.

"Nobody knows except you two outside of my own family."

"How do you manage that?" Jett asked.

"I don't let my employees get involved in my personal life."

I finished off my slice of pizza and washed it down with one of the sugary sodas that had come with the delivery. I usually preferred diet, but I made do. A woman had to save on calories somewhere, and I preferred to sacrifice my drinks rather than my food.

I watched silently as Jett and Marcus became involved in a discussion about cyber security, one of Jett's favorite subjects. I couldn't help but notice how closed off Marcus seemed, even though I knew he could be thoughtful when he wanted to be. I'd always seen him as arrogant, but some of his overconfidence probably came from being so self-contained. He'd spent most of his time traveling, so he'd only had himself to rely on, and he hadn't shared much about his personal mission to keep our country safe. It had to be hard to be unable to share so much of his life.

I knew exactly how he functioned because I'd spent so much of my own life exactly the same way. Maybe I hadn't been hiding the fact that I was some kind of roaming spy, but I knew what it was like to have to keep everything inside myself. Except for my brief affair with another correspondent who was more like a casual friend and acquaintance, I'd always been lonely. I'd just been too busy and focused to recognize those emotions. Or maybe I'd just never met anyone I really wanted to talk to about my travels except my siblings, and they had their own lives, their own interests.

I knew that the last person I should be attracted to was Marcus, but I couldn't seem to shake off the chemistry and emotional draw that I felt whenever I was with him.

He was actually dressed casually today, and the look suited him. His butt filled out a pair of jeans like I'd never seen them filled before. Marcus was hot, but there was so much more than just his physical appearance that made me want to fly close enough to his heat to get myself burned.

He might be here now, but he'll be gone soon. He's an international businessman who travels most of the time. I can't even think about getting involved with him.

My body wanted to say *yes*, but my common sense was screaming at me to ignore how much I wanted him.

I was still trying to figure out who I was after everything that happened to me during my kidnapping. Marcus was guaranteed to mess with my newfound sense of peace.

Maybe I wasn't the woman I'd been a year ago, but I was okay with that now. Life was full of heartache and change, and I was going through a period in my life where I just had to search for something new.

My first priority was to put away the man who was funding a group of terrorists so they couldn't hurt anybody else. My sense of justice wouldn't let me rest until I did.

"Dani?" my brother said in a loud voice.

I heard him, and I suddenly brought myself out of my own thoughts. "Yeah?"

"Did you hear me?" Jett asked, his voice concerned. "Are you okay? I asked you twice what you thought about Becker's motives for funding the rebels."

"Sorry," I answered. "I was thinking about something else."

I was busy daydreaming about crawling up Marcus's amazingly hard body and begging him to do me.

"What were you thinking about?" Marcus inquired.

"Nothing important," I said hurriedly. "So what did you want to know?"

"Becker's motives?" Jett repeated.

"He's never talked to me specifically about any of his illegal activities," I informed my brother. "But I think he's delusional. His motivation for everything is money, but I think he also wants power. In funding the terrorist group, I think he's under the impression it will give him control of the resources in the region if they can take possession of the area. Nothing else makes sense, and I've watched him pretty closely. Money and power are the most important things in life to him."

"He certainly doesn't value the women in his life," Marcus grumbled.

"No, he doesn't," I concurred. "They're just something he wants control over. Something he can use to vent his crazy anger on. I'm not a *person* to him. I'm a *possession.*"

"Fuck! I hate using you to get information," Marcus exploded. "It's insanity to think you might not get hurt."

"I might. But it's worth the risk to me. I've done plenty of risky investigative work, Marcus."

"I know. I've seen you in action. And it scares the hell out of me."

"Me, too," Jett added.

"I'm a grown woman," I argued. "I have been for a long time. I've been out there alone chasing stories for years now."

"I don't think either one of us doubts your courage, Dani," my brother answered. "Hell, I'm pretty sure that you were so confident that none of us even quite understood how vulnerable you really were. If we had, I think we would have put personal security on you."

"I would have gotten rid of them," I retorted. "One of the reasons I went blonde and tried to change my appearance was to disassociate myself with the billionaire Lawsons. Very few people even knew I was related to one of the world's richest families, and I wanted it to stay that way."

Just like Marcus, I didn't let anybody into my personal life. I wanted everyone to focus on the problems I was investigating and the story I had to tell, not my identity. My bylines on written articles were published as Dee Lawson, and I used the same name with my on-air reports.

I'd asked my network to use the name "D. Lawson" in the very beginning of my career, and they'd ended up printing it as "Dee Lawson." The moniker had stuck with me for the rest of my years as a reporter, making it less likely that anyone would recognize my unusual first name and immediately associate me with the wealthy Lawson family.

"So nobody ever really knew who you were?" Marcus questioned.

I shook my head. "Nobody really knew me. I was just some pushy American reporter to most people. My crew didn't even know."

The only individuals who were privy to that information were the human resources department of my network, and my bosses. Otherwise, I was just Dee. And that freedom had become important to me while I was climbing the ranks within the network.

"I knew you, Danica," Marcus answered in a hoarse voice.

"I know. I was always afraid you'd give me away, but you never did."

We'd pretty much ignored each other, or we fought when we were out of earshot of other people. In many ways, I'd tried to push him as far away from me as he could get.

"You could have told me. I never would have outed you," Marcus answered in a curt tone.

"You never did anyway. We barely spoke to each other."

My brother stood up and tossed back the last of his soda before he said, "I'm out of here. I want to go dig up as much dirt on Becker as possible."

I got to my feet, too. "I should get going."

Jett had left the room when Marcus asked in a low voice, "Why do you have to leave? Do you have a date?"

I knew he was concerned about me meeting up with Becker again. "I'm not going out with Greg without telling you."

"Somebody else?" he asked as he followed me to the door.

"So what if I do?" I asked him irritably. "What does it matter who I see if I'm not going out with Greg?"

He put his hand on the door as I went to open it and then pinned me into a small space by placing his other hand on the wall. "It matters," he answered simply.

I looked up at him, my body trembling with need as our gazes met in some kind of heated battle that I didn't quite understand.

"Does it?" I asked in a husky whisper.

"Yeah. It does. Don't see anybody else, Danica."

"Are you afraid Greg will find out?"

"Screw Becker. I don't give a damn what he thinks. I don't want to see you with another man."

I wasn't sure what he wanted from me, but his eyes were blazing with fire as he held my gaze.

His masculine scent assaulted my senses, and my pulse started to race. I finally answered him with a breathless tone that had nothing to do with fear. "I have to go…do laundry."

Okay, that was probably a lame excuse for leaving like my ass was on fire, but I was confused, and I knew I couldn't take much more of Marcus's presence without wanting to get him naked.

As my words sunk in for him, he started to smirk. "In that case, I have some dirty shirts that need to be done."

I shot him a fake, sunny smile. "Then I guess you're going to be busy tonight, too," I answered in a smart-ass tone. "Good night, Marcus."

I pulled on the door, and he finally removed his powerful hold on my exit. He leaned down before I could open the door, his warm breath wafting over my ear, causing me to pause with a shiver. "As soon as you leave, I'm going to take a shower so I can get myself off while I think about every dirty thing I'd like to do to you. I can't look at you without getting hard. I never could," he shared in a smooth-as-good-whiskey voice that made me crazy.

"Thanks for sharing," I answered nervously, knowing I was going to be thinking about the exact image he'd just brought to my mind, and it was going to last all night long.

Marcus...

Naked.

Wet.

Hard.

Stroking himself while he thought about doing dirty things to me.

Straining as his body finally found release.

Heat rushed between my thighs. "I hate you for doing that," I informed him.

"No, you don't," he countered. "You're turned on and we both know it."

"Dream on," I said haughtily as I pulled on the doorknob and rushed out the open door, unable to keep trading barbs with him when all I wanted to do was strip off his clothes and climb his body like it was a tree.

As I hurried to the elevator, I heard a sound that was completely foreign to me.

It took a moment for the noise to connect to its source for me.

It was Marcus Colter's wicked laugh.

Chapter 13

Dani

I was busy for the rest of the week.

Marcus and Jett insisted that I move my clothes and belongings to Marcus's condo just in case I got caught and needed to hide out after my meeting with Gregory Becker.

Actually, most of the orders were coming from Marcus, and over a space of several days, I found out how careful, cautious, and annoyingly anal he could be. I knew the fact that he was covering all of his bases came from his years of gathering intelligence for the CIA, but he wasn't exactly subtle about what he wanted. When he "suggested," what he actually meant was for me to move my ass and do whatever he wanted. Even though being bossed around grinded on me, I respected his experience, so I complied gratefully, wondering why I'd never thought about or planned for some of the things he mentioned.

Probably because I've never been a spy. I was sure Marcus's life depended on him being anal about planning.

"Are you really ready for this, Dani?" Jett asked nervously as I stood in the living room of my condo Friday night, ready and dressed exactly the way Greg liked.

My brother and Marcus had come to the house as soon as it was dark, only entering after they'd verified that I wasn't being watched.

Jett's concerned tone made my heart ache. Even if I *wasn't* ready to try to get information from Greg's home, I wouldn't let Jett know it. He'd been through way too much himself to worry about me. If I showed the slightest hint of hesitation, I knew my brother and Marcus would cancel the entire mission. "I'm fine. I think that Marcus more than covered any possibility," I answered confidently, yanking on my tiny red skirt so it completely covered my ass.

"No, I didn't," Marcus said stoically. "Nobody can ever be ready for everything. But we've taken some measures to ensure that you're safe."

My cell phone rang in the tiny clutch I was holding, and I dug into the bag, worried that Greg was calling to cancel.

But it wasn't Becker.

"It's Ruby," I told Marcus, turning away to answer the phone, stepping toward my bedroom where Ruby wouldn't hear the two guys in my condo.

"Hey Rubes," I answered cheerfully.

We'd spoken once earlier in the week, and she'd been safe. I'd called Marcus after the conversation, letting him know that I had to get Ruby out of the bad situation she'd fallen into.

"Dani," she replied in a relieved voice. "It's tonight. The auction is tonight. The people taking care of me just called. They told me to shower and to shave. Everywhere."

My heart fell. I had been hoping I could swing by and get her out of her hotel tonight, right after my last encounter with Becker. That had been my plan. The moment I was finished gathering information to bust the bastard, I'd have no reason *not* to pick Ruby up and get her to a safe place.

"Where is it happening?" I asked breathlessly.

"I think it's some kind of underground club right down the street, from what I could get from conversations. Dark Satisfactions is the name of it. I heard people talking here. That's all I know. They're coming to get me, and to make sure I'm completely shaved. I get why they're doing it. I might be a virgin, but I'm not stupid. They cater to kink."

I was more than certain that the club did indeed cater to unusual preferences, and they wanted Ruby to appear as young as possible.

Jesus! What in the hell was I going to do? I turned and looked at my brother and Marcus. As I remembered how much info Jett had been able to get on Becker, I was struck with an idea. "Jett!" I said urgently, holding the phone away from my mouth.

My brother broke off his conversation with Marcus to answer, "Yeah?"

"Did you see any information on Dark Satisfactions when you were looking for info? It's an underground club."

He nodded. "Connected to Becker, but in a convoluted way. It's on the dark web."

The club's connection to Becker wasn't really a surprise. I'd always suspected he was involved with Ruby's plight in some way. I lifted the phone again to tell Ruby, "Don't argue with anything they want. We got the location, and I'm sending somebody to help. Please trust me. I won't let anything bad happen to you. Can you believe that?"

The line was silent as Ruby seemed to contemplate what I said. Finally, she answered. "Right now, you're all I have, Dani. You're the only hope I've got unless I get a chance to escape."

"Not a hope, sweetie," I assured her. "I'm sending you a sure thing. But don't make them hurt you by trying something crazy. Somebody is getting you out of the auction site safely."

"Okay," she answered, her voice reflecting a spark of faith.

I knew she had no real reason to believe in anyone, and she had no reason to trust. I had no way of showing her that not everybody wanted to exploit her, or hurt her, except by showing her that some people were worth putting her faith into.

I hung up and then approached Jett. "I need you to be a hero tonight," I informed him. "Please. I need your help."

He frowned at me. "I'm always willing to help you, but I'm nobody's hero."

"You will be tonight. I need you to work your way into Dark Satisfactions and help a friend. It's not just a sex club. They're human trafficking, Jett. At least in Ruby's case." I was fairly certain there were more, and we needed to close down those businesses completely.

I explained to my brother and Marcus quickly, knowing I was short on time.

"Jesus, I hate this prick even more than I did before," Jett cursed. "I'm on it. I'll get her out of her situation, and then we can go to the authorities."

I put my hand gently on my brother's arm. "She's scared, Jett."

I'd just told him about Ruby's history, but I wanted him to understand that she might not trust him.

He nodded. "I doubt she'll be threatened by me. I limp, and she could outrun me right now if she wanted to."

I hugged him, so damn grateful that he had such a huge heart. "Be careful."

He hugged me back and then looked at Marcus. "Take care of her," he warned his friend.

"No worries about that," Marcus affirmed.

Jett only took a moment to pull everything together and he was out the door.

"He'll be fine," Marcus assured me. "He's probably one of the smartest guys I've ever worked with in any capacity."

"But his injuries are still going to be a disadvantage," I argued.

"Less than you think," Marcus drawled. "He might limp, but he's pretty damn strong. And sometimes brains are more important than brawn. I need you to focus on what we're doing. Jett will be fine."

I nodded. "I'm ready."

"Not quite yet," he denied, reaching his hand into his pocket to pull out a chain and a pendant.

I didn't stop him when he went to drape the piece of jewelry over my neck and then pulled my hair from the gold chain.

"What's this?" I asked uncertainly, fingering the cameo pendant.

Marcus flipped the pendant over. "Since Becker is a paranoid prick, I don't doubt that he isn't going to let you keep your cell phone for pictures. This is a backup."

"Are you telling me this actually takes photos?" The pendant was relatively tiny.

He demonstrated how it flipped open, where the button to take photos was, and how to use the device, and then closed it again. "It takes very good photos as long as you do exactly what I told you to do."

"How is that possible?" I questioned.

"I'd tell you, but then I'd have to kill you," he said in a mocking tone.

I shot him a tremulous smile. "Highly classified?" I asked.

"Actually, yes. And so is this." He pulled something else out of his pocket.

"What?"

He slid a simple beaded bracelet over my wrist. It was plain, and like the pendant, it was nothing flashy. I was guessing it was supposed to be nondescript so as to not draw attention.

He adjusted the beads carefully as he said, "Touch the beads, but don't twist them."

I put my index finger carefully on the cool, artificial stones. "One of them is smooth," I mused.

Marcus quickly explained how the pepper spray device worked. It was pretty simple. With a quick, powerful twist to the smooth stone, a high concentrate of pepper spray released into an assailant's eyes if one's aim was good.

"Aim well, and make sure you have an escape route," he advised. "If you don't move your ass, you'll end up getting some of it yourself. Don't do it in an enclosed area or if you can't get away."

I marveled at some of the nifty gadgets that Marcus had access to. "Got it," I acknowledged. "What? No matching ring?"

"No, but I have earrings," he mentioned casually, drawing a pair of plain black stones out of his other pocket.

I was wearing a pair of dangle earrings that matched my white shirt, but he motioned for me to take them off, and I ridded myself of them quickly.

"Do I want to know what these do?" I asked as I threaded both wires through my pierced holes.

"Press the inside button on either one of them and the signal comes directly to me," he explained. "And you'd better use it at the first sign of trouble," he grumbled.

"Panic buttons?" I asked.

"Don't wait until you panic," he advised. "Once you think he might be onto you, push the damn button. I'm going to be on your ass anyway, but I need you to signal me if there's a problem."

Nice as all these tiny tools might be, what really touched me was the fact that Marcus Colter looked worried.

"Hey," I said softly. "I'll be okay."

His staunch expression didn't soften as he snaked a hand around the back of my neck. "You better be. Don't take any chances, Danica. Promise me."

I glanced up at him, meeting his tumultuous gray eyes. My heart skittered as I saw the strain on his face. "I won't. I promise."

"I must be fucking crazy for helping you do this," he rasped.

"I'm crazy," I corrected. "You're just watching out for me."

"That seems to be a job I do well," he said hoarsely as his head lowered to capture my mouth.

I couldn't help but sink into his hard body, opening for him as he demanded my submission. I wrapped my arms around his neck, losing myself in his strength for a moment, allowing myself to feel.

I'd steel myself for my meeting with Becker as soon as Marcus let me go, but for just an instant, I needed to feel protected, and the only one who could make me feel less alone was the man who was holding me like he never wanted to let me go.

Chapter 14

Marcus

It had been the worst kind of torture to watch Dani get in her car and drive away.

Yeah, I was following behind her in a very ordinary sedan, but I knew I had to keep my distance, and I hated it.

I should have pulled her out of this whole thing. What in the hell was I thinking?

I'd questioned my own sanity several times over the last few days. Usually, I'd use whatever contacts I could get with a threat to national security, and Becker was definitely dangerous because of his enormous funding of the rebels.

But *she* was no ordinary contact.

And the way I felt leaving her at all vulnerable was downright insane.

I didn't want her with Becker. I didn't even want her in the same city with him. Yet, I needed her to help me gain access to critical information, intel that would finally bring Becker down for good.

Jett had made incredible progress by "digging" for dirt on Becker on the dark web, but not quite enough to present to the necessary departments to take him down. Hell, Becker had so many offenses it was going to be hard to figure out *who* was going to handle *what* on government offenses. But that wasn't my concern.

I wanted to bust Becker on so many levels, but the sense of protecting our country from foreign governments or terrorists was ingrained in me. What I wanted the most was to take Becker down for good. After that, I wanted the whole damn organization that had harmed Dani to cease to exist and not be a threat to our goddamn planet.

Everything I was insisted that I let Dani get access to intel. I'd been using any method necessary to impede anybody who wanted to harm the US in any way. However, as a man, I was having one hell of a time watching Danica be some kind of sacrifice.

"I'll get her out quickly," I muttered, still trying to convince myself that I was doing the right thing.

In theory, one person for a nation was a fair trade-off.

But that wasn't at all how I felt right now.

If Becker caught Dani in action, or doubted her loyalty to him, he'd kill her without a second thought.

"Fuck!" I exploded, slamming my hand on the steering wheel. My only consolation was that I had various departments of the government to back me up, even though I *technically* didn't exist for the CIA.

I wasn't an employee.

Nobody had a file on me.

The information I gained was put in investigative files, and my involvement quickly disappeared.

Just the way I liked it.

However, I'd helped enough starched shirts in the government that I could still call on plenty of people for help, including the FBI and some of my fellow CIA agents.

I watched as Dani pulled into a driveway ahead of me, and I stayed back, parking some distance away and cutting my headlights.

Now wasn't the time to second-guess myself. I needed to keep my head on straight and think like a spy.

She had every available gadget I could get my hands on to both protect her and help her stay undetected. Yeah, I broke out in a sweat as I watched her exit her compact vehicle in a skirt so short that she had to yank it down to cover the cheeks of her ass. It wasn't that I didn't appreciate the look. But I didn't want any other guy looking at Dani the same way.

As usual, she'd done her makeup way too heavy, but she was just as damn gorgeous as ever, and I coveted her, wanting to keep her all to myself.

As she disappeared into the luxury home, I had to admit to myself that she was the gutsiest female I'd ever encountered. She'd never flinched in trying to bring the world international news, and she hadn't broken under the captivity of men who had tormented her in every way possible.

Now, she'd thrown herself into danger again. Maybe she was wary, but she was determined.

The moment I'd met her, I'd wanted to nail her against the wall. But the way I craved her now was at a whole different level.

Mine! She's fucking mine.

It took all I had not to get out of my damn car and go find her, take her away from anything that could possibly harm her.

Problem was, she was the most stubborn woman on earth.

I drummed my fingers on the steering wheel impatiently as I felt my cell phone vibrate in the pocket of my jeans. I'd dressed for comfort and mobility, trying to make myself as ordinary as possible.

My eyes never leaving the house, I pulled out my phone and answered it. "Colter," I said abruptly into my cell.

"Marcus? Everything okay?" Jett asked, his voice solemn and low.

"Just got here," I replied. "She's in. I'm just keeping the house under surveillance."

"Damn," Jett cursed. "I hate this."

"Me, too, buddy," I admitted. "How is it going there?"

"Good thing I'm worth billions," he scoffed. "Gaining entry into the club is exhaustive and expensive. But I'm in. The auction starts shortly."

"Whatever it costs, I'll pay you back," I told him with no res-ervations. Ruby was Dani's friend, and we had to get her out of harm's way.

"Oh, hell no. If I'm going to buy a virgin, I'm paying for it," he replied. "I'm doing this for my sister. And maybe a little bit for Ruby, too. Jesus. She hasn't had the easiest life."

Dani had explained to me and her brother how Ruby had gotten into being a victim of human trafficking. "They always pick the most vulnerable," I told Jett in a disgusted tone.

"Yeah, well, it's bullshit," Jett said adamantly. "What sick indi-viduals do this shit?"

"People like Becker and his minions," I drawled.

"They don't just sell virgins," Jett replied. "There's all kinds of illegal crap happening here, and I don't think the majority of women who are present here, are here on their own free will or working willingly."

"The place has to get shut down," I told him. "Just get Ruby out without looking obvious, and we'll let law enforcement handle it. Get as much information as you can."

"Ruby will probably have to testify," Jett said in a regretful tone.

"She will. But hopefully she'll be so happy to escape that she'll do it."

Jett hesitated before he said, "I gotta go. Take care of my sister."

"I always have," I reminded him.

"You have," he acknowledged. "Probably more than she ever real-ized. I have a feeling you've always had an eye on her in some way or another. Even when she didn't realize it."

I wasn't fessing up to his claim, even though it was true. "Maybe," I answered noncommittally.

"Does she know how you feel?" Jett asked.

"What?" I asked innocently. "She's like a sister to me, too."

Jett snorted. "I call bullshit, buddy. But you can sort that out later if you're not ready to deal with it. Just keep her safe."

"I plan on it," I responded grimly.

We talked a minute or two more, shaping up our plans for later, and then hung up to focus on our objectives.

Jett was taking Ruby back to my condo, but if everything went smooth, I'd have Dani's ass on my private jet as soon as she was out of Becker's place. I had people moving our belongings to the airport and onto my plane.

I didn't want her anywhere in the area when all hell broke loose.

Chapter 15

Dani

I would be lying if I tried to convince myself I wasn't afraid.

But while I was trying not to flinch under Becker's intense scrutiny, I did have the security of knowing that Marcus was outside, waiting for a signal if I should get in trouble.

I was determined that this man I'd been tailing for weeks wasn't going to slip away from prosecution. He was a traitor to my country, and pure evil in every other respect.

I tried not to show my aversion to him as he roughly stroked my cheek. "I've been waiting for this night, Dani."

I'm sure he had been. The night that he'd left me black and blue was still fresh in my mind every time I looked at him. Women were nothing more than disposable trash to him.

"Me, too," I murmured, not being totally untruthful. I was, in fact, waiting for him to get his ass nailed against the wall.

I was grateful for the tools Marcus had given me since Becker had taken my keys and my handbag the minute I walked through the door and stashed them somewhere unknown. He was paranoid, but it had been a move I wasn't expecting.

"I need to go freshen up," I told him as I rose from my place beside him on the couch. I had to find my way around his home, and just being so close to the man who had cuffed me so hard I still had a faint outline of black-and-blue marks on my face made me slightly nauseous.

"Hurry up," he insisted in an annoyed tone. He stood up and took off his suit jacket as he added, "I've got plans for you."

I smiled weakly as I shuddered, not even wanting to know what his plans might be.

"Be right back," I answered sunnily.

He jerked his head to the left. "The bathroom is at the end of the hall. Stay out of the other rooms."

"Okay," I answered meekly as I turned away and scurried down the hallway.

I closed the door to the toilet loud enough so he could hear it, and then leaned back against it.

Damn! How was I going to get anywhere when he was watching me like a hawk?

"I can do this. I can do this," I whispered over and over like it was my mantra.

Problem was, I'd seen the ugly, violent side of Gregory Becker, and it had scared the hell out of me. I'd seen the same expressions when I'd been brutalized by my kidnappers.

Lifeless.

Dead.

Emotionless.

Where there was no conscience, there was no hesitancy to hurt, maim, or kill.

I had no doubt that just like my jailers in the Middle East, Becker enjoyed causing people pain and misery. In fact, I was pretty sure he excelled at it.

I pushed myself off the bathroom door, catching my reflection in the mirror as I moved. My white blouse was nearly transparent, but I was wearing a white sports bra underneath. I looked like a hooker trying to attract a man with layers of makeup and bright-red lipstick.

The frightened expression in my eyes just wouldn't do. No matter what, I wasn't cowering down to Becker. I was playing a role that would get me what I wanted.

I turned my back on the mirror, my mind racing. I thought I'd seen what looked like a home office on my way to the bathroom. It made sense that it was located on the ground floor.

The home was beyond pretentious, the décor opulent but decorated with gold, a fact that told me that he felt like he had something to prove. Everything I'd seen so far was downright gaudy and over-the-top.

I flushed the toilet to make it sound like I'd actually used it, and to drown out noise as I gently twisted the doorknob and opened the bathroom door enough for me to escape.

I didn't hear anything from the living room as I slipped into the open door I'd seen on my way to the bathroom. Moonlight bathed the room in dim light.

I rushed to the desk and flipped on the small desk lamp, listening for any trace of footsteps coming down the hallway.

Quietly, I opened all the desk drawers, looking for any sign of paperwork.

Dammit! Nothing!

I was ready to give up when I spotted a bookshelf next to the desk. My heart was pounding as I saw a large ledger that seemed out of place right next to some of the classics.

I pulled out the large, untitled book, and then opened it on the desk.

Bingo!

It was a book of transactions, illegal money being sent through various shell companies and offshore accounts to hide the income from his darker businesses. I didn't think; I just started using the tiny cameo Marcus had given me to get records and names of the companies.

I moved as quickly as possible, snapping as much information as I could in a short period of time. The amounts and dates weren't as important as capturing the names of the companies and the accounts.

I was amazed by the fact that Becker hadn't even bothered to try to hide exactly where the money was coming from. It listed the human trafficking, prostitution, and drug deals right in the ledger.

Maybe he was too arrogant about covering his tracks. He's obviously done it for years. Nobody has even dug deep enough to follow the money.

I was just replacing the large book when I heard footsteps.

"What in the fuck are you doing in here?" Becker said, his tone furious.

I moved my hand slowly. "I was just admiring your book collection. You have some great classics," I lied, thinking quickly about how to cover myself.

Dammit! I'd almost made it out before he came after me.

"I told you not to go anywhere except the can," he said in a surly tone.

I cringed as he moved to my side, the fury in his expression terrifying.

"What else were you doing? Bitch, are you spying on me?"

"Of course not," I answered in an innocent tone. "I just like books."

"So you just happened to stumble in here?"

"Yes."

"Bullshit," he exploded. "I hate liars, and you're not telling me the truth."

"I am. I swear I am," I answered in a pleading tone. "Why else would I be here?"

"I don't know. Why don't you tell me?" he demanded.

I startled as he grabbed a large hunk of my hair, yanked my head back, and I felt cold metal against my face. Out of the corner of my eye, I verified what I already knew. He was holding a gun to the side of my head.

"Tell me!" he bellowed. "What in the hell were you looking for?"

"Nothing. I just stopped in here because I could see the bookshelf."

I swallowed hard, trying not to think about the weapon aimed at my head.

Keeping his grip on my hair and the gun close to his target, he pushed me in front of him. "Move," he said in a menacing voice, pushing me to set my body in motion.

"Where?" I asked, trying not to let my fear take over.

"We're going to take a fucking ride. I don't trust you here."

My heart was racing as I stumbled over my high heels in front of him, his grip on my hair feeling like he was tearing it from my scalp.

Marcus! Signal for Marcus.

There was no way I was getting away from Becker's death grip. If I released the pepper spray, there was no guarantee he wouldn't shoot me on the spot.

The only way to get help was to bring Marcus into the mess I'd just created. But I was terrified he'd get wounded or end up dead. There was no way for me to warn him that Greg had a gun.

I hesitated as Becker pushed me outside and toward his vehicle in the driveway, trying to think about how I could pull myself out of the situation without getting Marcus hurt.

As ordered, I climbed into the passenger seat from the driver's side, his weapon trained on me the entire time.

"You'll pay for your betrayal, bitch. Nobody snoops around me and lives to tell about it," he bragged as he got into the driver's seat.

"Greg, I wasn't snooping. I was just looking at your office," I said, trying to reason with a madman.

"I told you what to do, and you had to go digging around. I said to stay out of the other rooms. You brought this on yourself."

Sweet Jesus! He was so paranoid that I wasn't going to be able to reason with him.

He pushed the button to start the vehicle, and I started to contemplate whether or not I should push the panic button for Marcus's backup.

By now, he'd probably seen us. The house was sheltered, but if he was on the street, he might already know what was happening. If he came into the situation knowing Becker had a weapon, he might be more careful.

My thoughts instantly dissipated as the lights in the car came back on, and Becker was temporarily diverted by a man standing next to the open driver's side door. The gun that he had trained on me wavered for a moment, and it only took me seconds to figure out why.

"I'm taking this vehicle, asshole. Get out or I'll blow your head off," Marcus growled in a low, agitated tone.

Like Becker, Marcus had a gun, and it was leveled at Becker's head.

Like I was watching in slow motion, the weapon moved from being aimed at me and started toward Marcus.

With a twist of a stone, I hit my mark with the pepper spray in my bracelet. A wounded howl escaped from Becker's mouth as I grabbed for his gun.

Marcus moved faster than me, grabbing Becker's shirt and hauling him out of the vehicle, and then slamming him to the ground as he intercepted Becker's gun in the process.

He hopped into the driver's seat and sped away, making sure he had the keys in the vehicle before he left Becker's bellowing figure on the ground.

I fumbled for the control for the windows, opening the one on my side as fast as possible because of the discharged pepper spray.

I panted for breath, my heart galloping as I realized that I'd escaped with Marcus.

"What are you doing? Where are we going?" I asked in a panicked tone.

"Not far," he answered in a clipped tone.

We stopped a few blocks away from Becker's house. "Are we getting out?"

"Get into my sedan. Go!" he said in an urgent tone.

I stumbled out of the luxury sports car and to the vehicle I'd seen Marcus driving earlier in the day. I'd barely closed the door when he stepped on the gas and sped away from the abandoned vehicle.

I didn't speak as Marcus drove. My body was still shaking, and I was still trying to figure out what the hell had just happened.

Marcus had appeared out of nowhere, and I'd definitely been looking for any sign of him when Becker had brought me outside.

Everything had happened so fast. All I'd been able to process was the fact that Becker was trying to shoot Marcus. I'd acted completely on instinct when I'd released the pepper spray.

Finally, I said in a husky whisper, "You're safe. We're both safe."

"I could have used some help before you used the chemicals," Marcus said tightly. "If you were in trouble, why didn't you signal for me?"

It was a reasonable question. I just wasn't sure how to answer.

Chapter 16

Jett

I'd done some crazy-ass shit in my life, but what was happening before my eyes was one of the weirdest things I'd ever seen.

I watched as a naked woman left the stage, obviously happy that her body had fetched a high price, judging by her smile. Apparently, not *all* of the women here were victims, but I had no doubt many of them were either brainwashed or coerced into the situation.

Jesus Christ!

What female would want to be sold like their value was nothing more than monetary? Probably not many.

I'd done some bad things in the past, usually to save lives or keep people from getting hurt. I'd done plenty of illegal hacking. I'd even used a gun to fire on terrorists when I was working with Marcus for PRO. I might have been the tech guy, but every one of us had been skilled with weapons of all types.

But I'd never—in my wildest damn dreams—imagined the atrocities that were happening here at this club tonight.

My body stiffened as I realized the grand finale of the evening, the virgin sale, was about to occur.

I heard men talking in hoarse whispers as a naked woman stepped into the spotlight on stage, and then my heart completely stopped.

The woman looked young, probably barely drinking age—if not younger. I had no doubt that this was Ruby, and I already knew she was almost twenty-three years old, but she looked like she could be straight out of high school. Her body was youthful and curvaceous, her pussy obviously shaved to make her look even younger than she did naturally.

For fuck's sake, even her hair was in two ponytails at the side of her head, and she was completely devoid of makeup—not that she needed any.

She was beautiful in a totally earthy way. But her expression was what was making my heart do strange things that it had never done before.

Her head was held high, but I could see the fear in her eyes. I'd gotten a table near the stage, and I could see her swallow hard as she tried to gather up the courage to keep her chin up.

She was trembling, even though she was trying to wrap her arms around herself to try to stop it and hide it. When the man holding onto a thin chain around her waist knocked her hands away from her body to put her on better display, I had to keep myself from jumping onto the stage and strangling the bastard.

The MC's voice sounded over the loudspeaker. "What would you give to get this pretty young thing into your bedroom? She's one-hundred-percent virgin, and ready for whatever you have planned for her. Or maybe you prefer a dungeon where you can torment her slowly before you take what you paid for. A prize like this is worth any price. She's afraid, and I have a feeling she'd put up a good fight. Imagine punishing this one for being a naughty girl. Gentlemen...let's start the bidding."

My gut rolled. *Jesus!* I had to admit I'd been around the block, and I could be as kinky as the next guy. But this was *way* too difficult for me to be comfortable observing.

The young woman looked hopeless, and I was almost feeling her pain and humiliation.

I tried to catch her eyes, but she was still staring straight ahead, her head up like she was trying to salvage her pride.

I frowned as I looked closer, noticing that she was biting her lower lip.

Protective instincts surged up inside me, the need to save this woman from further pain and humiliation so strong that I had to force myself to stay in my seat.

The bidding was ridiculous, a slow torture that I almost wanted to just end by offering any price for her.

Stay cool. Stay calm.

I looked around the room, watching some rich old men practically salivating to get their hands on the woman gracing the stage.

Hell, I wanted her, too. I wasn't innocent. But I was more desperate to rescue her than I was to fuck her at the moment.

I didn't want a terrified female.

All I wanted was a woman who actually wanted *me* now that I was damaged goods. But Lisette had already taught me a lesson about wanting more than I could ever have.

I was damaged, and there was no way in hell I was ever going to find anybody who didn't cringe at my scars. Hell, sometimes they even made me look away from the injuries on my own body.

I signaled to the auctioneer—if I could really call him that—to up my bid.

I wasn't leaving the building without Ruby.

The bidding hit six figures, and men started to slowly drop out with disgruntled looks. The amount of money being offered was nothing to me. I had more money than I could spend in plenty of lifetimes. I didn't care if we hit seven figures or beyond.

I had no more than placed my bid when I suddenly looked up and met Ruby's gaze. Her steady, tormented expression made me want to just scoop her up, wrap her in something warm, and take her home with me.

I knew something about her life, things that Dani had shared with me.

She was a woman who'd never really known kindness.

She was a woman who'd usually been cold, defenseless, and alone on the streets.

She'd been hungry.

She'd been frightened.

And by God, I was going to show her that not *all* people were bad.

Ruby deserved a whole lot better than the crappy hand that life had dealt her.

I sent her a conspirator type of wink and a grin. I was rewarded by the first hint of emotion from her dark and tortured eyes.

For just an instant, I saw a glint of hope pass across her face before it fled just as quickly.

Dani hadn't told Ruby exactly how she'd help her, but I was hoping she'd understand that the last thing I wanted was to hurt her.

Finally, Ruby was going once.

Going twice.

Sold—to the gentleman in the front row.

I breathed a damn sigh of relief.

Ruby was coming home with me.

Chapter 17

Dani

"Marcus, is this big rush really necessary?" I asked as I fastened my seat belt for takeoff in his massive jet. "Yes," he answered simply.

Okay, he was angry at me for not signaling for him to come and help me. Maybe I should have explained that I was terrified that something would happen to him, but I'd made up some stupid excuse instead.

He hadn't liked my explanation.

So, he'd been nearly silent while he'd driven like a bat out of hell to the airport.

Honestly, the whole carjacking idea had been brilliant. The ruse and the lack of connection between me and Marcus had been perfect. I'd already handed over the tiny camera to a government official who had taken it when we'd arrived at Marcus's jet, and left almost immediately to have the information analyzed.

If they could get what they needed, Becker *would* go down. If Greg thought Marcus was simply a carjacker or a thug, then he wouldn't really get twitchy about the fact that someone might be onto him. He'd be most likely to believe the criminal who'd taken the car and the woman inside the vehicle had gotten cold feet when they found me in the car and both of us had bailed. Or at least that's what I hoped he'd believe. It would give law enforcement time to do what was needed to arrest the jerk.

I knew we were headed to Rocky Springs. I'd heard Marcus talking to the pilot. "I don't even have a home in Colorado," I informed him.

"You'll be staying with me," he replied in a voice that allowed no argument.

"Do I have a choice in this decision?"

"No," he answered flatly.

"And will you continue to be pissed off at me?"

I could have mentioned that I had a sister in Colorado, one I could most certainly stay with when I arrived. However, I could tell now wasn't the time to be argumentative with him.

Marcus was…well…*he was Marcus.* That meant he was bossy as hell, which could be incredibly annoying. But it was hard to get angry at a man who kept saving my ass.

"Most likely," he grumbled.

"I wish you *wouldn't* be," I shared. "You saved my life tonight."

"Again," he said in an ornery tone.

Granted, he *had* saved my butt twice now. And I was grateful. But I didn't want to spend the whole trip to Colorado with him in a mood. "Thank you," I said, putting a hand on his arm in gratitude.

"Don't thank me. I'm beginning to think it's my goal in life to make sure you stay alive."

The fact that he cared enough to keep saving me was actually humbling. Marcus was one of the richest men in the world, and he had a lot on his plate. He didn't have to worry, but he did. It said a lot about his heart and the kindness that was buried underneath his sarcastic and gruff exterior.

"I didn't want Becker to hurt you," I said in a rush. "I was afraid because he had a gun. I didn't want him to take you unaware and have you end up injured or dead because of me."

Marcus was silent for a moment before he said, "If I ever let somebody take me unaware, I'd be dead by now. For God's sake, Danica, it's not like I didn't know that asshole didn't have more than one gun."

"I couldn't risk it," I told him as I removed my hand from his arm.

"You should have," he argued. "*Christ!* I'd never get over it if something had happened to you. It would have destroyed me."

My heart tripped as I realized his anger was all for me, generated by his fear for my safety.

Oh, Marcus. You're a better man than you know.

Maybe he was formidable, but the guy had a good heart.

"I was willing to take the risk," I reminded him.

He turned his head and pinned me with his steel-colored stare. "I wasn't," he growled. "I hated this whole damn idea from the beginning. Did he hurt you?"

I shook my head slowly, mesmerized by the volatile emotion I could see in his gaze. "No. Not really."

I could feel the jet leveling off, and the seat belt sign went off.

"I have to use the bathroom," I said as my head began to spin.

I fumbled with the restraint and then stumbled to my feet.

Marcus steadied me. "Are you okay?"

"Yeah," I muttered. "I'll be fine."

I used the seats for balance as I sprinted toward the toilet. Once I'd closed the door, I lowered the toilet seat and sat down.

I'd gotten there just in time.

Sweat beaded on my forehead, and my heart began to race until I was gasping for breath. A loud sound started to buzz in my head, and tears flowed down my cheeks. I put my hand on the counter by the sink, willing the helpless feeling to go away.

But it seemed like it lasted forever.

"Danica? Dani? What the hell is the matter?" I heard Marcus say, his voice muffled by the ringing in my ears.

I was swept up into my own dizzy, heart-pounding, breathless world for what seemed like an endless period of time before I started to come back down again.

"Dani!" Marcus called to me, demanding that I respond.

Problem was, I couldn't say anything. Not until my body belonged to me again.

I put my trembling hand on my thigh, leaning over to get some air. I felt like I was choking, but I knew I wasn't.

Finally, the fog started to clear and I started to suck in some deeper breaths.

"I'm making an emergency landing," Marcus said emphatically. "I think we need to get you to a hospital."

As I came back into my body, I protested. "No. Don't."

He was kneeling in front of me, holding a cold cloth to my sweaty forehead. "I don't know what's wrong—"

"I know. Just give me a minute," I pleaded. I started to take deep breaths and straightened up, taking the cloth from his hand to wipe my perspiring face.

"You're getting some color back. Jesus! You were as white as a sheet. What happened?"

"Panic attack," I answered. "I haven't had a full-blown attack in a long time. I guess what happened tonight just brought it on. It won't kill me."

I was mortified that I'd fallen apart in front of him, but I'd forgotten that the bathroom had an entrance from the bedroom where he'd come in.

"You have panic attacks?" he asked gently. "Since the incident a year ago?"

I nodded as I started to feel steadier, my heart regaining its regular rhythm. "I thought I was over them. They were pretty bad after I got back to the States a year ago. Through therapy, I've slowly recovered from my PTSD and anxiety. But I guess I'm not quite there yet. I'm sorry."

He took my hands into his as he told me, "Don't be sorry for something you can't control. If the only thing you're left with is an occasional panic attack, you're doing well. Jesus, Dani. You've been through hell and back. Why can't you give yourself a break?"

"It helps to be busy," I said weakly.

"You can stay occupied with something safe," he said in a graveled voice. "How are you feeling now?"

"I'm okay now. I hate not having control when they happen. I feel like I can't breathe, I get really dizzy and disconnected, and my heart races about a million miles a minute. It's embarrassing, and I feel so damn helpless. My last experience with this was months ago. I've learned how to deal with them, but I guess it's still going to happen occasionally, especially if I'm stressed out."

"I'll help you. Just tell me what you need and I'll get it."

He sounded so sincere that it made my heart clench. "It's over. I'll be okay. I just need to take a shower and get out of these clothes."

I was fairly certain that the amount of sweat that had come from my body was making me stink.

"What can I do?" He started to pull my foot from my ridiculously high-heeled shoes.

"You're already doing it," I answered with a smile.

"What?"

"Help me get out of this outfit," I requested.

He tossed the shoes aside, straightened up, and then pulled me gently to my feet. "I'll stand by in case you get dizzy again."

"I don't think it will happen again. I don't get them that close together. But I'd still like your help." My hands were shaking as I started to unbutton my blouse.

Marcus batted my hands away and started to confidently release the buttons. "I'll do it."

"Will you take a shower with me, Marcus?" I wasn't really suffering any aftereffects other than being tired. Now that I'd released the stress I'd been burying, I was okay.

I'd learned through counseling that panic attacks weren't going to kill me, but a lunatic almost had snuffed out my life earlier tonight. Maybe it was the reminder of how fragile life could be that made me want to reach out and grab exactly what I wanted.

"Why? You said you'd be okay," he reminded me as he slid the blouse off my shoulders.

"Because I want you to," I confessed. "You asked me if I needed anything. The only thing I *really* need is you."

Chapter 18

Marcus

I wasn't sure I could see her naked and not want to fuck her.

Hell, I couldn't see her *clothed* and not want to nail her.

After she'd scared the shit out of me earlier tonight, and then just a few minutes ago while she was sweating bullets and gasping for breath, my need to be deep inside her was even stronger.

I hated the fact that she still had lingering effects from her time as a captive, but it was understandable. She'd been so damn brave, and I knew this latest investigation had to have affected her in a very big way.

I wanted to make her feel safe and protected.

Yet, I also wanted to see her coming for me.

She was offering, and I felt goddamn helpless to refuse. *But...* "Dani, I'm not going to take advantage of you right now. It's been a really stressful day. Our adrenaline is still running high."

I watched as she shimmied out of her skirt. "The way that I need you has nothing to do with adrenaline, Marcus. It's there. It's always been there. I've just tried to ignore it. But when I realized tonight that I could die in a matter of seconds, I understood that I have to stop being cautious sometimes. I have to ask for what I need."

She was right. Our instantaneous connection that had started years ago while we'd both been in hot spots had *always* been present. I'd wanted Dani for a very long time, but we'd both chosen to ignore it. Hell, I'd gotten to the point where I couldn't control my desire anymore, and I was damn sick of fighting it.

She was my best friend's sister. Dani should be off-limits. However, I was unable to deny her right now. "I don't want you to regret this," I said honestly.

Grabbing the waistband of my jeans, she said, "I'd never regret *you.*"

"This isn't going to be a fling for either of us," I warned. "We stay together and see where this goes from here. We aren't going to go our separate ways until both of us are ready."

"Okay," she agreed readily.

"We won't be able to go back," I warned.

"I don't care," she murmured as she released the most perfect pair of breasts I'd ever seen when she pulled the sports bra over her head and dropped it on the floor.

"Then fuck it," I rumbled, my eyes roving over her tight, curvy body that was now nearly unclad except for a pair of stockings and flimsy underwear. "I've never claimed to be a damn saint, and I certainly don't feel like one right now. If you want me, I'm yours."

"I want you," she answered almost immediately.

"Then God help us both," I said, scooping her up into my arms so I could carry her to the bed.

"I probably stink," she cautioned. "I was all sweaty."

"You don't," I assured her. She smelled as sweet as sin to me.

The angst between the two of us dissipated, and I could think of nothing except how damn right it felt to have her body against mine, skin-to-skin.

I lowered her onto the bed gently. I had to make sure I didn't move too fast. "Have you been with anybody since those bastards raped you?"

I was pretty sure I knew the answer to my question, but I had to ask her anyway. If I was the first for her since the kidnapping incident, we had to take things slow and easy.

"No. I didn't want anybody else. I'd only been with two guys before, and nobody since I was raped by the terrorists. Now, the only man I want is you."

Shit! What in the hell could I say to that? I was glad I was the first guy she'd wanted in a long time, but I was also wary that she wasn't yet ready to be with someone.

I shucked off my jeans and dropped them onto the floor. "Dani, are you sure you're ready for this?"

My dick was already plenty hard, but it got even firmer as her eyes roved over my body like she wanted to devour me.

"I'm beyond ready. Please, Marcus," she pleaded in a vulnerable tone.

I dropped beside her and then hovered over her as I met her needy gaze. "Jesus! You're so damn beautiful," I told her hoarsely.

I shuddered as she put her hands on my chest to stroke the muscles there and then moved to my biceps.

I stopped for a moment, just absorbing the feel of her hands on my body. I'd wanted this for so damn long it was almost surreal. Finally, I lowered my head to kiss her.

The minute she opened to my demand, I *knew* I was fucking lost. I'd lusted after this woman for so damn long that my body was tight from holding back.

I took everything she gave me, and then I asked for more.

Finally, I lifted my head and buried my face in the side of her neck, feasting on the tender skin as I heard her moan. All I wanted to do was explore her beautiful body, make her moan louder.

"Marcus," she said in a breathless voice as I latched on to one of her nipples, determined to make sure she was spoiled for any other guy except me.

Mine! She was always supposed to be mine.

I listened and watched her reactions carefully, not wanting to put her into a panic. There was no way I was *not* going to savor this experience, but my dick was urging me to hurry it along.

"This feels so good, Marcus," she said, her voice quivering.

"It's about to get a whole lot better," I replied, straightening up for a moment so I could remove the thong she was wearing.

She helped, lifting her ass as I dragged the small piece of silk from her body.

Damn! One wrong move and her ass would have been hanging out of her short skirt. All she'd have had to do was bend the wrong way.

"I have a love/hate relationship with these," I rumbled, tossing the panties off the bed.

I heard her stifle a laugh, and I was pretty sure she knew exactly what I was thinking as she said, "Do you want me to take off my stockings?"

They came almost to the top of her thighs, and were secured by a black, lacy band.

"No," I decided. "Leave them."

I ran a hand up each of her thighs, loving the hell out of the silky feeling of her stockings, but it was so much better when I hit her satiny-smooth skin.

She jumped, but she didn't shy away as I lowered my body between her thighs. My heart was racing as I explored the small band of sensitive skin above the stockings with my thumbs and then edged up to plunge a finger through her silken heat, parting her folds, only to be met by a wetness that made me catch my breath.

Christ! She really does want me.

Her pussy was wet, moist, and more than ready for my insistent cock. But I ignored it. What I really wanted was to taste her, devour her juices until I was satiated.

I heard her whimper as I buried my face between her thighs, tasting every inch of her sweet pussy with a flat tongue and subtle pressure to her clit.

"Oh, God. Marcus. Yes."

Her desperate words were followed by a hard grip on my hair, urging me to make her explode with pleasure.

I took my time, slowly ramping up the tension in her body by giving her more and more stimulation to the tiny bundle of nerves that I knew would get her off.

Her hips rose, the move done solely to try to get her satisfaction. She ground her hips against my mouth, silently urging me to give her more.

I got drunk on the taste of her, and the erotic movement of her hips grinding up with every stroke of my tongue.

She was desperate as she panted, "Make me come, Marcus. Please, make me come."

I didn't want to stop, but I could hear the strain in her voice, and the last thing I wanted was to confuse her. There was time enough later for delayed gratification. For now, I just wanted to give her everything she wanted.

I focused on the little pulsating nub, my tongue stroking over it hard, allowing Dani to fly a little higher.

Her grip on my hair intensified, and my mouth grew rougher and rougher as I heard every catch of her breath.

Come for me, Dani. Come on. Let go.

I stayed on her clit, but I used my other hand to penetrate her sheath, using one finger to open her, and then two to fuck her.

She was writhing beneath my mouth, her breath coming hard and fast, when I felt her body tighten. A strangled scream left her lips when I felt the inner walls of her channel clamping down on my thrusting fingers.

"Yes. Yes. Yes." Her chanting was incoherent, and I'd lost any other words she might have spoken. All I could hear loud and clear was her acceptance of her oncoming orgasm.

I was sweating bullets as I imagined her tight, slick sheath taking my cock.

Her muscled sheath clamped down on my fingers, and her body began to tremble as she rode her climax full force. Her back arched off the bed, and her hips ground up, her fingers clutching my hair with a death grip.

I lapped at the released stream of juices as they flowed from her pussy, savoring every single drop.

"God, Marcus. What in the hell was that?" she exclaimed as her body started to spiral down.

I moved up her body slowly. "I believe it's called an orgasm," I informed her.

"I've *had* orgasms. I give them to myself. That was...different."

I tried like hell not to think about her getting herself off. It was a picture that would now probably be perpetually ingrained on my brain.

I plopped beside her as she caught her breath, moving one of my slick fingers to her lips. "This is what you taste like," I growled, watching as her mouth opened and then clamped onto my finger.

My dick twitched, imagining that sensual mouth taking something other than one of my digits.

She sucked on my finger for a moment before releasing it. "Amazing," she said simply.

I smoothed her damp hair from her face. "Yeah, you are," I replied, deliberately misunderstanding her meaning.

She was so responsive.

So ready for me.

So damn fearless.

I kissed her forehead as she recovered her breath and then flopped onto my back. Every instinct in my body wanted her, needed to fuck her and make her mine.

But my protective instincts intervened, saying maybe I'd pushed her as far as I dared for now.

Chapter 19

Dani

My eyes were closed, and I felt like my body was so sensitized that I could feel every breath I took entering and leaving my lungs.

What Marcus had done, and the way he made me feel, had completely blown me away. I'd entered a world of pure, sensual pleasure, and it was a space that I never wanted to escape.

"That was..." Hell, I had no words. I wanted to tell Marcus how I felt, but how do you say thanks for something you never knew existed? "Orgasmic," I finished in a hoarse whisper, knowing that what I'd said was lame, but not knowing how else to describe it.

I had some previous sexual experience, but nothing had ever felt like *that*. The pleasure had been so intense that it was *almost* painful. The fact that Marcus had seemed to enjoy every moment of the experience had made it just that much more powerful.

I slowly recovered, and then noticed that Marcus was flat on his back.

Rolling to my side, my head propped on a pillow, I asked, "Is everything okay?"

His arm was covering his eyes. "Yeah. I'm good."

He didn't sound *good*; his voice sounded beleaguered.

"What's wrong?" I pressed.

He rolled to his side so we were face-to-face. His fingers threaded into my hair as he said, "Nothing is wrong. Seeing you like that was fucking amazing."

Marcus was being honest. I could see it in his eyes.

"Then why are you waiting? I'm recovered, and there's nothing I want more than you," I told him hesitantly.

He let out a masculine sigh. "I still remember how scared you were when I kissed you on my jet right after you were rescued. Dani, I don't ever want to see that look on your face again."

I propped myself onto my elbow. "Wait a minute. You think I'm scared?"

He moved with me, putting his hand beneath his head. "Aren't you? You still have panic attacks, Dani, and you haven't been with a guy since you were gang-raped."

A tenderness for this man beside me flowed over my body and landed in my heart. He was afraid for me, worried about me not being ready to have sex again. "Marcus, I wouldn't have started this if I didn't want to finish it. I'm not afraid of you," I informed him in a gentle tone.

"You should be," he grumbled. "The crazy-ass way I want you scares the hell out of me."

I knelt beside him, running my hand down his muscular abdomen, and then reaching inside the elastic waistband of his underwear for what I really wanted. "I can tell that you want me," I teased, stroking my fingers up and down his rock-hard shaft.

"Jesus Christ, Dani, knock that shit off before you find yourself underneath me and at my mercy," he growled, his jaw clenched tight.

I tugged on his boxer briefs, pulling them off his body by sheer will, because he didn't help me one bit. His body tensed as I straddled him and then speared my hands through his hair and lowered my body down on his, savoring the way we felt skin-to-skin. I kissed his forehead before I put my lips next to his ear. "Fuck me, Marcus.

Do it before I go crazy. I *want* you deep inside me. I want to watch *you* come."

I knew he was fighting his desire, and I was determined to make sure he lost. His concern for me touched my soul, but there was no need for it. I wasn't a fragile flower, and I had never, ever been afraid of *him*. Maybe time hadn't healed all of my wounds, but I wasn't afraid of sex or Marcus. Really, all I wanted was sex *with* Marcus.

Maybe if it had been anyone else but him, I might feel differently. But it was *him*, the guy my body desperately craved, and I wasn't fresh from the rescue anymore.

I knew what I wanted.

I knew what I needed.

My problem right now was trying to explain to him that I wasn't going to be afraid.

No way was he going to leave me again like he had in the restroom.

I sighed as his fiery skin warmed my body. I ground down against him, hoping he'd finally get the message, while my lips trailed along his cheek and then to his mouth.

I kissed him hard, letting him know I couldn't get enough of him, and my body caught fire as he finally responded. His fingers dug into my hair, pulled me closer, and then explored my mouth with a desperation so thick that it was nearly palpable in the air around us.

When I lifted my head, I warned him, "If you don't fuck me, I'm *taking* what I want."

"Do it," he rasped. "There's no way I can resist you. I have no damn idea how I've done it for this long."

I wasn't about to wait any longer now that I knew that he was with me. I slid back, positioning myself to take him inside me, and then lowered myself onto his cock. "Oh, God, Marcus. I've wanted this for so long," I whimpered as my muscles stretched to take all of him.

"Keep going, baby. Take me. All of me," he demanded.

I smiled as I completely seated myself on him, my body screaming with happiness as I finally got what I needed.

Marcus's hands slapped onto my hips, gripping them hard as he thrust his hips up.

I sat up and put my hands on his shoulders, moaning as I felt him straining into me.

"Don't hold back," I pleaded, knowing that I needed him so desperately that slow and easy wasn't going to cut it.

He eased my hips up, and I caught his rhythm. Beads of sweat formed on my face as he gave me more, our bodies meeting with a satisfying slap every time he guided me down again.

"Marcus," I whined helplessly, my head falling back, my body demanding the fulfillment he was promising.

"You're so fucking beautiful," he grunted, his powerful biceps flexing as he kept thrusting into me.

Harder and harder.

Over and over.

Both of us working our bodies together like they belonged this way.

Something hot slithered through my belly and started to ripple outward.

"Come for me, Dani. I'm not going to be able to hold back much longer," he rumbled, one of his hands coming off my hip to slide his fingers to the place where we were fused together.

The first rough stroke over my clit sent me reeling.

The second made me climax, my orgasm hitting me like a fast-moving bullet train. "Marcus. Marcus."

I couldn't do anything except call out his name, my body shuddering as I completely imploded.

I fell forward again, and our slick bodies slid together as Marcus held my hips, his cock pummeling into my sheath with an urgency I could feel even as I reached my peak.

"Dani. Baby," he groaned in a sexy, throaty voice. "Fuck!"

My channel was clamping down on his thrusting cock, and I savored the expression on his face as I dove down to kiss him, knowing I was milking him to a hot release.

His embrace was rough and hard, a passionate expression of the way we were both letting go and just feeling ourselves go up in smoke.

I welcomed his heavy, masculine groan as he released himself inside me, my entire body trembling as my climax hit its peak, and then started to wind down again.

"Holy fuck!" Marcus cursed, wrapping his arms around my body to hold me safely against his chest.

I was panting, and my heart was galloping so fast it was almost impossible to discern the separation of the beats. One flowed into the other, and a profound sense of peace like I'd never known washed over me. "I've needed that for so long," I said in a stunned whisper.

Maybe I'd tried to hate him.

Maybe I'd had to constantly remind myself that I knew he was a dog because of what I'd thought had happened with my sister a decade ago.

Maybe my attraction to him had always been there, but I'd never acknowledged it.

But thinking back honestly now, I couldn't remember a time when I *hadn't* wanted Marcus, no matter how much I'd tried to deny it.

He wasn't safe, and he probably wasn't what I *should* be needing. That was probably why I'd never allowed my conscious brain to think about the heat that flamed between the two of us.

I might have buried it in anger and resentment, but what had just happened had been a very long time in the making. The desire he could conjure up inside me just by being close to me had *always* been there.

"I know, sweetheart," he answered huskily, his hand stroking over my hair in a comforting motion. "Me, too."

Of course our attraction was mutual. It wouldn't have been as explosive if it wasn't, if we didn't both have the same chemical reaction to each other.

Having sex with Marcus was like playing with fire, but considering what had just occurred, I was willing to risk getting burned.

"I didn't use protection, Dani," he said remorsefully. "I was so far gone that I didn't think about it. I've never done that before."

"I'm clean," I reassured him. After all, I had been gang-raped over and over, so he had a right to be concerned. "And I'm on birth control. After what happened, I'll probably always stay on the Pill or some type of contraceptives."

"Hell, I'm not worried about you," he said in a coarse tone. "But you didn't ask about me."

"I don't need to," I told him.

"Why?"

"Because I know you well enough to realize that if you weren't clean, nothing would have happened without a condom," I explained.

"I'm not a saint," he denied. "But I'm clean. I've never had sex without a condom before, and I get checked regularly."

"So I'm your first?" I teased.

"My only right now," he said.

My heart turned. I'd love to be Marcus's only for a while. "I stink," I told him with a sigh. "But I'm not sure how I'm going to get up and into the shower. I think my legs are too weak."

He sat up and moved to the edge of the bed, taking me with him with one arm wrapped around my body. Then, he lifted me up, forcing me to put my arms around his neck as he stood.

"What are you doing?" I squealed.

"Taking my weak-legged woman to the shower," he answered nonchalantly.

I squealed again as he hefted me higher into his arms and proceeded to take me to the shower.

I laughed until we finally got into the water. After that, Marcus and I were quite busy concentrating on other pleasurable activities.

Chapter 20

Dani

When we arrived in Rocky Springs, I did end up staying with Marcus. Not because he ordered it, but because I *wanted* to be with him.

Somewhere between my panic attack and our touchdown, I'd realized that no matter how much I tried to insulate myself, there was no guarantee of happiness. Honestly, I'd probably realized that truth during the time I'd been a prisoner of the rebels. I was going to have to make a play for what I wanted in my life.

And if I didn't at least try to make Marcus part of my future, I was only going to be going through the motions.

I was in love with him. *Completely. Totally. Irrevocably.*

And if we couldn't be together for the rest of our lives, I'd cherish every moment I had with him.

"I have to admit, I thought we'd end up fighting over you staying here with me," Marcus said as he started stripping off his clothing in the bedroom of his Rocky Springs mansion.

We'd caught almost no sleep on our journey back to Colorado, and we were both ready to get some rest.

"It's almost three a.m.," I reminded him. "And I'm feeling magnanimous."

He grinned at me from across the room. I'd just slipped on a nightshirt from my suitcase, and he was taking off his clothes so fast that it was nearly mind-boggling.

I'd had a brief tour of the house before we'd retreated back to the master bedroom.

Still smirking, he asked, "And why is that?"

"Because I got what I wanted," I purred, smiling back at him. "That does tend to mellow me out."

"What a coincidence. I got what I wanted, too, and I didn't have to throw you over my shoulder to get you to my place when we got home."

"I *want* to spend time with you," I confessed. "I don't want to crash at Harper and Blake's house. They haven't been married that long."

"Then it's a good arrangement for both of us," he drawled, coming toward me as naked as the day he was born. "Because I want to be with you, too."

Even though I was exhausted, I couldn't help but admire his amazing body and the way he moved. He reminded me of a predator stalking prey.

"Come with me," he insisted, holding out his hand.

"I already did that on the plane," I answered in a teasing voice, and then placed my hand in his.

"Smart-ass," he answered, sounding more amused than irritated.

"Where are we going?" I asked curiously, letting him lead me to the French doors that I assumed went out to a patio since the master bedroom was located on the first level of his house.

His home was huge, but it managed to be massive without being incredibly pretentious. I loved the high ceilings and the modern décor, something that seemed congruent with Marcus's personality.

"You'll see," he answered mysteriously, swinging open the doors. "I haven't had time to do this for a while."

The large patio area was enclosed, but the top of the outbuilding was open. "This is beautiful," I told him in an awed tone.

The gardens were colorful, but tasteful, and the flowers were gorgeous.

When he finally stopped walking, I swept my eyes lovingly over the incredible hot springs in front of us.

I'd grown up near Rocky Springs, but the Colters had the large majority of hot springs in the area. The resort featured pools both large and small, but I was betting on the fact that each sibling had built a house near a private pool. Hell, I would if I owned their property.

I could smell the minerals, but the scent was pleasant, and highly tempting. He'd kept the natural look, the pool sided by rocks with ledges and a lovely waterfall.

"Are we getting in?" I asked hopefully.

"I thought maybe you could use it to relax," Marcus answered off-handedly, trying to pretend like he wasn't being the most thoughtful guy on the planet.

He slipped in first and then held his arms out for me to jump down beside him. Without a second of hesitation, I leapt into his arms.

"Oh, God," I moaned as the warm water hit my body. "This is incredible."

"I'm glad you like it," he answered.

He took a spot on an underwater rock and pulled me to sit between his legs.

"Did I really scare you when I had that panic attack?" I asked curiously. God knew I'd tried to run off and hide it. I knew watching me freak out probably wasn't a very pleasant sight.

"Yes," he answered simply.

"I haven't had one in a long time," I explained as I looked up at the stars. "But I hate the fact that I never know when and how it's going to happen."

"Why now?"

I shrugged. "I think it was probably the stress of dealing with Becker. And before you scold me, I wasn't going to back out. So don't even go there."

"Well, shit," he grumbled.

I knew he'd *so wanted* to go there, telling me he should have done something different.

"Marcus, it was something I had to do. I'd been holding Becker's name in my mind for months. When I finally remembered that the terrorist had mentioned him as a source of their funding, I knew that stopping him was something I needed to do."

His arm tightened around my waist. "Why? You could have just taken the information to the authorities."

"Then what?" I questioned. "I couldn't prove anything. You told me he'd been successfully running dirty businesses for a long time, and he'd never been arrested. This was personal to me. A lot of people have been hurt or killed because he funded the rebels and had some kind of delusion that he could rule his own territory on the other side of the world."

"I understand," he finally conceded. "I might not like it, but I get it."

I returned to our original subject. "I'm in counseling. I have been since the whole thing happened. I never miss an appointment because I want to feel normal again. If necessary, I do a video chat with my therapist. I've resolved a lot of things, but there's some areas where I'll always be different than I was before it occurred. I thought my panic attacks were gone. Maybe they were, and this is just a setback."

"Can you take it easy for a while?" he grumbled.

I smiled into the darkness. "Maybe."

"What else is different?" he asked.

I sighed. "Everything and nothing. I'm still the same person, but I feel like I just view *life* differently. I know how easily it can end now, and I don't want to take anything or anyone for granted."

"I want you to stay safe," he said huskily. "My heart can't take any more of your adventures right now."

It was amusing that a man like Marcus was talking about his supposed vulnerabilities. "Someday, I'd like to go back to the Middle East just to prove to myself that I can. I want to know that my courage is greater than my fear."

"It is," Marcus rumbled. "Believe me, it is."

"I never used to be afraid of anything," I said with a touch of sadness for the woman I used to be. "Now I have to fight to get rid of my fear."

"You're the bravest woman I know," Marcus argued. "Have you ever heard the quote that goes something like this—*I learned that courage was not the absence of fear, but the triumph over it.*"

"*The brave man is not he who does not feel afraid, but he who conquers that fear,*" I said, finishing the quote. "I think Nelson Mandela is responsible for that version of a very important point. But sometimes I'm not sure I'm actually triumphing."

"You *are* conquering your fear, Dani. You *have* succeeded in spite of what happened. It's only been a year. Be patient with yourself," Marcus said in a hoarse voice.

"I try," I answered. "I really do."

"It's okay not to be perfect," he stated. "I've known competent businessmen who have crumbled during a hostage situation. Hell, they never want to leave their house again."

"I'd go nuts," I confided. "But I'd really like to have my life back. I'd like to have *me* back."

"You'll get there," Marcus said. "Hell, you're already ballsy enough to make me nervous."

I let out a small laugh. "The great and powerful Marcus Colter? I doubt that."

"I'm still just a man, a guy who can't stand to see you struggling with everything that occurred. It never should have happened in the first place."

I leaned back against him, my heart clenching from the remorse in his voice. "It *did* happen, but it isn't going to keep ruling my life," I answered in a determined voice.

"You're fine just the way you are," he said assertively. "Everybody is afraid of something."

"What are you afraid of, Marcus?" I asked curiously.

He was silent for a minute before he answered, "Someday, I'll answer that question. But I can't right now."

"Okay." I wanted him to share things with me, but not unless he wanted me to know. For now, I was good with just enjoying our time together.

I had no idea how many days we had before he left to travel for business, but I was going to relish every moment we had.

"So what kind of recommendations did your counselor make? I trust he or she is knowledgeable about your particular situation."

"She is, and we take things one issue at a time. Her advice was to get a dog," I told him jokingly.

"Why?" Marcus asked, obviously confused.

"I told her I'd like to set down some roots, even if I still have to travel. I mentioned to her that one of the worst parts of traveling is being alone. I've always wanted a dog, but I never got one because my life was too chaotic. There would never be enough time for me to spend with an animal."

"You like dogs?" he asked.

"I love them. All breeds. I haven't met a canine that I didn't like."

"So get one."

"We'll see," I answered noncommittally. "I can't get one until I decide where I want to put down those roots, and how much I plan on being home."

"What else did she suggest?" Marcus questioned.

"A very long vacation. Catching up on my reading and movies, or anything else that doesn't involve traveling for work."

"Good advice," Marcus said approvingly. "You'll find everything you need right here."

Honestly, I had no idea how long Marcus and I would hang out together, but I wasn't against taking my vacation in Rocky Springs. I just hoped I didn't end up regretting it.

Chapter 21

Dani

It took a few days for us to get the news that Gregory Becker had finally been arrested. Some of the information I'd been able to obtain had finally tied him to a number of crimes.

Ruby was fine, staying with Jett in Florida for now to give her statements as a key witness to the human trafficking charges.

It made me feel good to know that at least something I'd done in the last year might prevent Becker from hurting anybody else. I would have preferred to move quicker, but Marcus was always there to remind me that I'd been responsible for putting the last nail in Becker's coffin, no matter when it had happened.

The bastard was finally off the streets and unable to finance rebel troops.

I'd quickly finished my investigative exposé and turned it in to my old boss, giving my previous employer a pretty big scoop. The article had just been published as the news about Becker had come out today.

I was in Marcus's office, a room that was masculine and stuffy, but reminded me so much of the man who owned it. Strangely, over the last few days, I'd started to like his extremely dry humor and previously annoying arrogance. He'd finally decided he didn't *have* to wear a suit and tie when he wasn't working, even if it *was* a workday. And if he was somewhat aloof and haughty, they were qualities he'd needed to do the things required of him by his company and his country.

He could be teased out of his autocratic tendencies, and he occasionally even had the ability to laugh at himself.

Okay…the laughing at himself wasn't all that common, but had happened a few times in the last couple of days.

One important thing I'd discovered is that no matter how hard he blustered, Marcus loved his family, and he cared about far more things than he'd ever let on. I couldn't say that I'd learned *all* of his secrets, but I *was* on to him. There was so much more to him than what a person could see with a casual acquaintance. He just usually chose not to show what was beneath the surface.

Maybe he had no idea how to really relax, but then, neither did I. We were learning together, seeing what it felt like to just take some time off. Granted, we used a lot of that time having sex, but we'd also played a few games of chess, caught up on movies we hadn't seen, and I was experimenting with cooking. Yeah, maybe I wasn't ready to become a chef, but Marcus's mom had stopped by yesterday to help me fix a casserole I'd totally screwed up. Luckily, she was willing to give me a hand learning basic cooking skills. Surprisingly, I was learning to enjoy cooking and baking now that I had some time and was in one place for more than a day.

I scrolled down the full-page piece I'd written on my laptop, satisfied to see my name as the byline. "It's live," I told Marcus excitedly.

He was behind his massive oak desk, dressed casually in a gray polo shirt and a pair of jeans. I was seated on the comfortable leather couch in his office with my computer.

"I know," he drawled. "I'm looking at it now."

Smart-ass. I should have known he'd find it before I did. It was kind of sweet that he was actually looking. "It was good," I stated without any kind of arrogance. I was a good writer and reporter, and it was no great accomplishment that I was able to push out a good piece when I had a decent story.

"It was fantastic," he corrected. "You're talented, Dani. I've always known that. Your correspondent stories were always brilliant. You have a knack for taking the perfect approach to any subject."

I looked up from my laptop and saw his broad smile. My heart skittered as I absorbed his compliment. It meant a lot coming from a guy like Marcus. He wasn't the type of person who threw out praise very often. "Thanks," I said, smiling back at him. "I'm glad it's all over."

"What are you working on now?" he asked curiously.

I shrugged. "Nothing important. Mostly my personal journal."

"And what do you journal about?" he pushed.

"Whatever I feel like writing," I answered. "Right now, I'm writing down my bucket list."

"Don't you think you're a little young for that?" he asked with a frown.

I shook my head. "Not at all. I thought I was going to die when I was a prisoner. It's funny what happens when you feel that way, and how many silly little things you regret not doing."

"Like what?" he asked huskily.

I'd gone to college right after high school, and then spent the majority of my adult life chasing stories in the Middle East. "Silly stuff," I evaded.

"Tell me," he insisted. "Maybe I've done some of them and I can tell you if doing any of those things are worth it."

I evaluated my list. "I've never built a sandcastle on the beach. I've never actually spent any time on the ocean. It was one of the many things I thought about while I was a captive."

"Never done that," he replied. "Never spent much time on the beach. I spent plenty of time flying over them, though."

"I've never been bungie jumping or zip-lining," I continued.

"Me neither," Marcus admitted. "Both of them are pretty dangerous—"

"Says the man who spies as a hobby," I finished.

"Makes more sense than jumping from a bridge counting on a big rubber band to save my ass," he grumbled.

I bit my lip to keep from smiling. "I think I can cross out the 'learn to cook' item off the list. At least I have been trying."

"What else?"

"I've never been drunk, not even a little," I confessed. "I was too busy in college trying to do everything I could to try to get hired as a journalist when I graduated."

"Done it. You aren't missing anything," Marcus rumbled. "Hangovers suck."

"Do you think going into the hot springs naked qualifies as skinny dipping?" I asked, my eyes on my list.

"In the water. Outside. Naked. Yeah, I highly recommend that one, especially if you're there with a beautiful redhead who makes you crazy."

I rolled my eyes at him. "I was with a handsome, dark-haired man who drives me insane. Will that work?"

"For now," he said agreeably. "Go ahead and remove that one. Tell me the rest."

"They're personal," I said hesitantly.

"You don't want to share?" he inquired, sounding slightly hurt.

"Okay," I agreed. "But they're kind of silly."

"Read them," he demanded.

"I've never kissed a man in the rain. I've never had a guy who really loved me. I've never been proposed to. And I've never had a child."

"You want kids?" he asked in a low, inquisitive baritone.

I shrugged. "Someday. Yeah. I never really thought about it until I got kidnapped. I guess those are the things you think about when you know your life might be over so early. Did I make the right choice? Did I put enough effort into relationships? Did I love my family and friends enough?"

Marcus leaned back in his leather chair, his entire attention on me. His eyes were intense, as though he was thinking about what I said.

"I can't say I know how you feel," he finally admitted. "But I understand reconsidering some of your choices in life."

"Aren't you doing exactly what you want to do?" I asked with surprise.

"Not always. I'm not as close to my family as I'd like to be, and I have no idea what I would have done for a career if I'd felt I had a choice."

"You didn't want to run your father's conglomerate?"

He shrugged. "I never thought about it. I was the oldest, and our father died young. He was killed in a terrorist attack—in the wrong place at the wrong time in the Middle East."

My heart clenched. No wonder he wanted to keep Americans safe. His own father had been a victim of unstable circumstances in a foreign country.

My mother and Marcus's had been friends. I knew his father had died, but I'd been too young to understand where or how it had happened back then.

Marcus continued, "As far as running Dad's conglomerate...I guess it was always assumed that I would. I was groomed for it, and it never occurred to me to argue. I know my mother would have wanted me to do whatever made me happy, but there wasn't really anything else I wanted to do."

"So you don't regret doing it?"

"I don't. I've become damn good at what I do. But I do regret the distance it's caused with my family. Hell, I don't even connect well with my own twin anymore. I told myself that I was doing it to protect them in case somebody found out about the government work I was doing, but I think I pretty much isolated myself because I knew I'd miss them if I didn't."

"Does that work?" I asked.

"Not really. It just makes the empty feeling easier to handle."

"Traveling around the world is hard," I commiserated. "Sometimes I'd be gone for months at a time on assignment. I missed my family a lot."

Marcus shrugged as he replied, "It was great when I was fresh out of college. But just like you, I wonder what I missed by not being here at home."

"No long-term relationships?" I asked. I couldn't even remember Marcus being linked with any one female other than my sister. That hadn't exactly been long-term, and that incident—as I now knew—had been a case of mistaken identity.

He shook his head. "No."

"Because you were traveling," I commiserated.

"I don't think that was the problem, actually," he corrected.

"Then what was it?"

He shot me a sharp look and then glanced back at his computer again. Still staring at the screen, he answered, "I guess I just never met anybody worth bothering to stay at home for until now."

Chapter 22

Marcus

I t wasn't that I didn't *know* I was completely fucked—I just didn't want to admit it.

I was hiking with Dani the day after she'd spilled some of her *list* to me, suddenly realizing that I didn't miss being on an airplane or in a foreign country at all. It was the first time I'd actually been stateside for more than a few days, and I wasn't the least bit edgy or eager to get back on my private jet and fly away.

I held her hand tightly as we both navigated down a rocky incline, worried as hell that something would happen to her. *Jesus!* I think I'd be fucking upset if she so much as broke a damn fingernail—not that she had long nails to break.

After everything she'd been through, all I wanted to do was protect her, make sure nothing bad ever happened to her again. I still had nightmares about seeing her right after her brutal captivity, and it wasn't something I wanted to see ever again. Hell, I didn't want to see her unhappy in any way.

Maybe she didn't see herself as strong, but she was one of the gutsiest women I knew. Honestly, she probably should have died while she had been held captive, but she'd pulled through it, and was still willing to risk her ass again trying to take down a man who was hurting other people. Danica's capacity to care about someone other than herself was probably both a curse and a blessing. Sometimes I almost wished she'd be more selfish, but then she wouldn't be Dani.

"I'm okay, Marcus," she said breathlessly beside me. We'd reached the bottom of the rocky area and had our feet on solid ground. "You can stop squeezing my hand. I'm not going to fall."

I released the pressure on her fingers, not even realizing I was holding them hard enough to cut off her blood supply. "Sorry," I rumbled. "I wanted you to have support if you fell."

"I won't fall," she promised, shooting me a happy, glowing smile as we trekked along beside each other.

Her grin made me feel like somebody had punched me in the gut. That's how I knew I was screwed. All she had to do was show any sign that she was happy and it had me thinking about how I was ever going to let her go.

Fuck that! She's not going anywhere!

The woman needed somebody to keep her out of trouble, and I was more than willing to volunteer for the job.

We were so much alike, yet so damn different. Neither one of us had ever put down permanent roots and let them grow. What I'd told her yesterday was the truth. I hadn't ever found anybody who made me want to slow down traveling.

Until her.

Until now.

Her sadness over things she might have missed if she actually *had* died made me want to help her experience every one of those items on her list. Sadly, I wasn't much help in telling her what was worth missing and what wasn't. My life had been as career-focused as hers.

Every moment I'd spent with her had been worth whatever I'd missed in my business life. I'd been overseeing my responsibilities from home, and very few things had needed my personal attention. My conglomerate had so much upper and middle management that they didn't constantly need me anymore. Everything ran just fine without me racing all over the planet.

Problem was, now that I'd experienced how good it felt to start being part of my family again, and I had Dani with me, I was afraid I'd grow to like the contentment way too much.

I was a loner.

I never stayed in one place for very long.

Hell, I wasn't even sure what I'd do with myself if I wasn't always on the go.

Right now, my focus was on getting Dani to relax and just be happy. She'd jumped out of one bad situation and into the next way too fast. There had been little time for her to recover, and it didn't surprise me that she'd experienced a panic attack after going so long without them.

I might not be the perfect guy to teach her how to relax. I wasn't exactly *Mr. Calm and Happy.* But I knew one thing…nobody cared about her well-being more than I did.

"Are you okay?" Dani asked quietly.

I shook myself out of my thoughts. "Yeah. I'm good."

"You were frowning," she pointed out. "And you looked like you were deep in thought."

I shook my head. "Nothing important."

Just me making a life plan for you in my mind!

Jesus! She was a grown adult. It was none of my business what she did in the future. We'd helped each other achieve a common goal: getting Becker put away for good.

Unfortunately, somewhere along the way, I'd stopped seeing her as just a cooperative journalist. Hell, I probably had *never* looked at her as just a reporter. There had *never* been a day when I hadn't wanted to nail her, and today was no exception. But there was a hell of a lot more than just sex between the two of us. We'd established a kind of intimacy that I'd never experienced with a woman before.

That was how I'd come to the conclusion that I was downright screwed, and I wasn't sure that I cared.

Being with her felt too damn good to worry about how involved I was becoming. But I probably knew, deep down inside, that I might end up regretting it. However, even knowing that I might end up completely alone and pissed off wasn't enough to deter me.

"It's raining," I informed her, suddenly feeling the light sprinkle that may or may not have been falling for a while.

"It feels good," she answered. "It was getting hot."

We were both dressed in jeans and a T-shirt. I'd donned a pair of underused hiking boots while Dani had slipped on sneakers for our jaunt.

"At least it's not storming," I replied. There was no thunder or lightning, and Dani was right. It had been getting warm.

"We're almost home, right?" she asked curiously, not sounding the least bit concerned.

"Almost," I agreed. I stopped in the woods, causing her to halt with me. "But it reminds me of something. It's on your list."

She looked confused for a moment, her puzzled expression and questioning eyes looking for clarification.

I nudged her backward until her body came into contact with the trunk of an enormous pine tree.

"Time for that kiss in the rain," I explained in a husky voice. "It was on your wish list of things you'd never done."

God, I loved the way she smiled and tilted her face up to absorb the raindrops falling from the sky before replying, "Yes, it is," she answered. "An experience you said you didn't know about yourself."

I shrugged. *What in the hell did I know about romance? I had quick fucks. I didn't get emotionally involved.* "It could be interesting."

She wrapped her arms around my neck. "We could try it," she told me suggestively.

When she swiped a bead of rain from her lips with the tip of her tongue, I nearly lost it. My cock strained against the denim material of my jeans as I grew transfixed by a pair of tempting lips that I couldn't resist.

"Make it happen," I insisted, bracing my hands on the massive tree trunk, one on each side of her head.

I wanted *her* to initiate the embrace. I had no fucking idea what I'd do if she didn't because there was no way I was turning back now.

I needed her too damn much.

Watching her eyes, I could almost see her brain working as she contemplated exactly what to do.

Kiss me, dammit!

For one long moment, I waited for her to act, my heart nearly galloping out of my chest as we simply stared at each other, both of us wanting the same damn thing.

Finally, she threaded her hands into my damp hair and pulled my head down.

Desperate, I met her halfway.

Chapter 23

Dani

Our lips met in a frenzied madness that I'd come to expect from Marcus, but I certainly hadn't gotten used to the emotions.

As usual, he took control almost immediately, and I opened for him with a reckless abandon that I couldn't deny.

Marcus was my weakness; the way he devoured me like I was the only woman in the world he wanted was way too tempting for me.

I moaned as his tongue swept into my mouth with a demanding strength that overpowered my senses.

I *wanted* more.

I *needed* more.

I was beginning to crave Marcus's touch in any way I could get it.

My fingers tightened on his hair, and I pressed my body against his, wanting to feel his hard body against mine. It was an obsession that I hadn't been able to tame. One that I didn't want to restrain because I knew he felt it every bit as much as I did.

By the time he lifted his head, I was frenzied. "Marcus," I murmured against his shoulder, feeling so vulnerable that I wasn't sure what else to say.

"You need me," he growled, lifting my head up so I could see the intense expression on his face. "Just like I need you. We both feel it, Dani. It's not just you."

It was remarkable how he could put into words *exactly* what I was thinking, and then put me at ease with those feelings by confessing that he felt the same way. I wasn't comfortable with my emotions being so exposed, but knowing he felt the same primal, out-of-control instincts made it easier to handle.

"I know," I said in a muffled voice as I buried my head against his neck.

I *did* comprehend that it wasn't just me, but it felt better to hear him say it.

I was disappointed when he stepped back, but my displeasure quickly turned to astonishment as he stripped off his T-shirt and tossed it to the ground. "What are you doing?"

He grinned at me, a mischievous expression that I was starting to adore. Maybe because I was pretty certain Marcus didn't show this side of himself often.

"Getting naked," he explained.

"Here?" I squeaked.

"Right here. Right now," he confirmed as he started to lift my T-shirt.

"We're outside in the rain," I reminded him.

"I know." He tugged on my damp shirt.

I lifted my arms and let him strip the T-shirt off. It might be raining, but it was still summer, and it was plenty warm.

"What if somebody comes?" I asked.

"Somebody *is* going to come," he answered nonchalantly as he continued to strip off my garments. "Hopefully both of us," he added.

I actually giggled as I watched him fumble with my sneakers, and I finally took pity on him by just slipping them off, and then stepped out of my jeans. "Feeling daring?" I asked as I used his shoulder to balance myself.

God, I loved this audacious side of him, his quiet confidence that he could do anything he wanted.

"Not really," he answered as he set my clothing aside on the ground once I was naked. "We're on my property. And I know that adding a little bit of intrigue gets you off."

His fingers trailed up my thighs, and I gasped, feeling something akin to an electric jolt surge through my body. It wasn't entirely comfortable, but it *was* arousing. "How do you know that?" I asked, already panting as his warm breath hit my naked pussy.

"Because I brought you to orgasm in a bathroom with somebody just barely out of sight," he explained with infuriating calmness.

"I was—" My voice cut out, and I completely forgot about protesting as Marcus's hands landed on my ass and his tongue speared through the pink flesh that was right in front of his face.

"Oh, God," I moaned, and then drew a sharp breath as that slick mouth started to mercilessly devour me.

I plunged my fingers into his wet hair, needing some kind of balance and sanity where there was none. I came undone as Marcus meticulously started his sensual campaign to drive me insane.

He drew my leg over his shoulder, forcing me to use the tree to keep myself upright, and to grip his scalp harder.

When Marcus demanded, I was nearly helpless *not* to respond.

He delved deeper into my pussy, his mouth, tongue, and nose all stimulating my sensitized flesh. His tongue lashed at my clit, and I trembled with need. My nude body was getting pelted by rain, and the most beautiful man on the planet was enthusiastically consuming my pussy like it was the only thing he needed for sustenance. It was the most erotic sensation I'd ever experienced.

I closed my eyes and drew my hands from his hair and then lifted them to grapple for a hold, finding it as I clutched the rough bark over my head.

Marcus teased, and then attacked. Savored, and then devoured with a hunger that seemed insatiable.

"Please make me come," I pleaded, my body quivering with the need to orgasm.

But he knew how to keep me from tumbling over the edge, to balance on a razor's edge, and it made me crazy. I'd start feeling the peak coming, and then he'd back off just enough to stop it from happening. Marcus was a master at forcing me into a state of desperate need.

"Marcus!" I screamed, not caring who might hear it. I *had* to come.

I tilted my head back as I felt the next wave building, Marcus burying his face in my pussy harder than he had before. Droplets of water from the sky continued to roll over my face and breasts, but I welcomed the sensual sensation. I was so lost in the pleasure of Marcus's mouth on my core that I couldn't think about anything else.

My fingers were gripped so tightly to the rough tree bark that I knew they were probably bleeding, but it didn't matter. I was completely focused on my need for release.

"Now," I demanded, but there was a needy tone in the command.

My climax washed over me so abruptly and forcefully that it was almost scary. I let out a moan of release and satisfaction, my body shaking as it was pounded by wave after wave of sensation. My orgasm was intense, and Marcus continued to lick and nip at the tender flesh, milking every ounce of pleasure he could from me, seemingly ravenous for every drop of my juices he could lap from between my thighs.

I panted as I tried to recover, my legs weak as Marcus gently placed my foot back on the ground.

"I hate it when you do that," I said breathlessly as he straightened and I wrapped my arms around him.

"No, you don't," he answered hoarsely. "You love it."

Lord help me, but he was probably right. I loved the anticipation, and the enormous release that only he had ever given me. Or maybe I had some kind of love/hate relationship with it. I loved the climax, but I hated the torment.

I love you.

In my emotional state, I wanted like crazy to say those words out loud, but I bit my lip to keep from crying them out.

"Maybe I like it a little," I admitted.

He pushed my hair back from my face. "You're wet," he said gravely. "Are you cold?"

"Are you kidding?" I snorted.

"Just checking."

I ran my hands down his muscular back, and they glided smoothly over the slickness of his skin. "Fuck me, Marcus. I need to feel you inside me."

He moved back enough to cup my breasts, teasing the saturated nipples with his thumbs. "I just want to watch you for a minute," he replied.

My eyes rose to meet his tumultuous gaze. "Why?"

"Because you look so damn beautiful right after you come. I like knowing that I was the guy who put that expression on your face," he answered covetously.

"Do I look ridiculous?" I asked hesitantly, not knowing that I had *that look.*

He lightly pinched my pebbled nipples and then ran a soothing circle over them slowly. I closed my eyes to absorb the pleasure/pain sensation as he repeated it over and over again.

He leaned forward and kissed my slippery lips before he said gruffly, "Hell, no. You don't look ridiculous. You look like you're fucking mine."

I moved my hands up his back and speared my hands into his damp hair. I had the same possessive emotions that he did, but it still clawed at my heart when he said something that *sounded* like he was claiming me. It felt primitive and feral, and it made me need him with a ferocity that I almost couldn't bear.

I reached down and fumbled with the zipper and button on his jeans. I needed him to fuck me so hard that I felt like we were somehow connected.

When my fingers finally brought out his enormous cock, I swiped the bead of moisture from the tip before the rain could wash it away and then brought it to my lips, watching his silver eyes glint with an emotion I couldn't name as I put my finger in my mouth and sucked it right in front of his face.

"I love the way you taste," I said in a sultry tone.

"Ditto," he answered in an aroused, raw, masculine voice as he lowered his head and met my lips.

I savored the taste of us together as he ravaged my mouth. It was dirty, but so damn intoxicating that I was clamoring for more.

I'd never really tapped into the sexual side of me until I met Marcus.

My hands slid down to grasp his cock, feeling it pulsate in my palm.

We were both soaking wet, and the rain was getting heavier, but Marcus and I were too lost in each other to give a damn.

When his mouth released mine, we were both panting. I savored the carnal look on his face as my palm slid over and over his cock in such a furious pace that he grabbed my wrist.

"Don't," he demanded. "I don't have a lot of patience left anymore."

"Then give us both what we need. Fuck me."

"I don't just need it, Danica. I have to have you," he said fiercely, his eyes molten with desire.

"Oh, God, Marcus. Sometimes I don't know how to handle this," I said, gasping for air as I yanked my wrist from his grip and wrapped it back around his neck.

I felt consumed.

I felt overwhelmed.

And the razor-sharp desire that was eating me whole was so confusing.

"Then don't think," he rumbled, pulling back for a moment to turn my body until my back was against his front, and he took advantage of the position by continuing his assault on my breasts. "Just let me fuck you," he added.

Every time his fingers tightened and released my tormented nipples, I let out a tiny gasp. His every touch was setting my whole world on fire.

He bent me over, helping me find my grip on the tree. His hands slid down between my thighs, urging me to part my legs more. I took a wider stance as I felt his eager cock press against the cheeks of my ass as he gripped my hips.

The ground around the tree sloped, putting him in the perfect position behind me. I waited, my head down and my drenched hair falling into my face again as I silently begged for him to fill me. The empty space inside me was demanding to be filled by Marcus.

When he surged forward, he wasn't gentle, and it was the first time he'd fucked me in this position. I wasn't used to the depth, and I squeaked as my tight muscles gave to allow him deep inside my slick sheath.

Right now, I needed Marcus's ferocity. He'd been careful and slow every time before today, probably because of my history of rape. But my body craved him, and there wasn't a single ounce of fear inside me. All I wanted was for him to take me hot and hard.

"Yes," I encouraged as my muscles relaxed and let him invade me until he was buried to his balls.

He leaned over my back, talking roughly into my ear, "Do you want it hard, baby?"

"Yes," I whimpered.

"Can you handle it?"

"Yes!" I was about to lose it. I needed him pounding into me before I went out of my mind.

He licked the raindrops off my neck, and then his teeth clamped down on my sensitive skin. It didn't hurt, but it made me even more desperate.

The heat of his chest on my back.

The way our skin slid together sensually.

The hot, dirty talk in my ear.

The sharp feel of his erotic nip to my neck.

All those things combined were a sultry feast. I shuddered with fierce desire. My entire being was clamoring for Marcus so badly I was ready to scream.

"Marcus. Please. Fuck me!"

He straightened up without another word, pulling back and then thrusting again with the same force.

I let out a sob of relief, my hips slamming back against him, my body greedy for every powerful surge.

He started a punishing rhythm that consumed both of us. There was nothing else except the meeting of our bodies.

I relished the pummeling of his cock inside me. It satisfied me like nothing else could.

There was only Marcus, and the pounding rain.

My hands were braced hard against the tree, and the rocking motion of my hips became more and more volatile as I felt the warm coil in my belly become an inferno.

"Harder," I moaned helplessly.

He gave me *harder* as he growled, "You're mine, Danica."

"Yes," I agreed in a fierce tone.

Right now, he owned my soul, and I didn't care. In fact, I was ferociously glad he did.

The coil in my stomach started to unfurl, and I braced myself for the onslaught as the sensation moved between my thighs.

Marcus took a hand from my hips and adjusted his position as he kept up his brutal pace.

I flinched in surprise as I felt his finger probing between my butt cheeks, the digit finding my anus, and our completely wet state allowing it to slide in a fraction without pain. The tight hole stretched, but he didn't invade. He just pumped in and out at a shallow depth, matching his finger to the pounding cadence of his cock.

I imploded, the new sensation causing a pleasure so intense that I couldn't possibly stop myself from climaxing, even if I wanted to—which I didn't.

This time, I let go, allowing my orgasm to wash over me as I completely embraced it.

"So good," I cried. "So damn good."

The muscles of my channel clamped down on Marcus's pounding cock, milking him to his own fiery release.

I absorbed the sound of his tormented groan, wallowing in it. As much as he seemed to like to watch me after I came, I loved to hear those sounds of intense relief and pleasure come from his lips.

He exited my body after a moment or two, swung me around, and wrapped his muscular arms around me. He cradled me, crooning comforting, nearly incoherent words as he stroked my saturated hair.

I let myself drown in his sweet words, feeling like the most cherished woman in the world.

When he'd recovered his breath, he did up his jeans, and he scooped me up.

"What are you doing?" I asked.

"Taking you home. I don't want you to cut your foot on rocks or other stuff on the ground."

I was barefoot. He was still wearing his boots. "You can't carry me all the way back to the house," I protested.

He *did* haul me all the way back to his house in his arms.

Granted, it was closer than I'd originally thought, but it was still far enough that no normal guy could make that trek with my weight as a burden. But when he reached the door of his home, he wasn't even winded.

I was beginning to learn that I should never tell Marcus he *couldn't* do *anything*, because he was stubborn enough to prove that he absolutely *could*.

Chapter 24

Dani

"**A**re you going to eat all of that?" Marcus asked later that evening as we watched the news, cuddled up on the couch in his living room.

I smiled as I took another bite of the massive hot fudge sundae I'd concocted just a few minutes earlier. I could hear the note of longing in his voice as I leaned back against him. My back was resting against the front of his body, a position that had become our favorite when we were relaxing together.

"I planned on it," I teased.

He didn't answer, but I already knew he was hoping I'd share. I'd already figured out that he didn't shun sugar and junk food because he didn't like it. He did it strictly because of his rigid discipline to stay healthy and fit for his travels. It wasn't that I objected. I understood that my obsession for junk food wasn't healthy. I simply didn't care. I ate healthy enough most of the time. A person needed some indulgences.

And lately, Marcus had been more than willing to allow himself some foods that were meant simply for pleasure.

My suspicion was that he could normally avoid it because he didn't see it, but since I devoured it on a regular basis, he was tempted. His mother, Aileen, was a phenomenal cook and baker, so I was certain he'd indulged plenty as a kid.

He wasn't nearly as snobby as he attempted to be about eating for pleasure.

Marcus could afford to consume what he wanted. He did one of the most brutal workouts I'd ever seen every morning in his home gym. I'd attempted to keep up with him, but had failed miserably.

According to Aileen, Marcus had loved chocolate when he was young, and I could tell that preference hadn't gone away. He just hid it well.

I pointed my spoon at the bowl. "This is really good. Are you sure you don't want me to make you one?"

"Nope. I'm fine," he answered.

Honestly, I think he liked junk food the best when he was eating *mine*. Maybe he could rationalize that because he didn't actually eat his own.

I sighed as I took another bite, the explosion of hot fudge and creamy French vanilla ice cream in my mouth absolutely perfect.

"I'd probably be willing to try a little of yours," Marcus rumbled, his low voice vibrating against my back as he looked over my shoulder.

I smiled broader, finally hearing him request to eat some of mine, just as I'd predicted. In fact, I'd been waiting for it.

"I'd hate for you to force yourself," I said in a false concerned tone.

"I wouldn't be," he contradicted quickly. "I really don't mind."

It was as close as Marcus was going to get to admitting he desperately wanted some of the ice cream masterpiece I'd made for myself. Since I knew he was going to want some, I'd heaped a lot in a very big bowl.

I turned, gathered the perfect bite in a spoon, and then held it up to his mouth.

"What do you think?" I asked after he'd quickly taken it from the utensil I'd offered.

He nodded. "You were right. It's really good."

I shared the entire bowl with him, amused that it was the only way I could really get him to eat something he enjoyed.

My body was exhausted from our earlier hike and subsequent passionate encounter outdoors. We'd showered when we'd come in out of the rain, and then had some dinner. Now that we'd slowed things down, I could feel the so-worth-it aches in my body from the volatile way we'd come together.

My fingers were scratched, something that Marcus had fussed over when he'd seen them in the shower. I was pretty sure he'd asked me at least ten times if they hurt.

They didn't.

And I didn't regret a single moment of experiencing my first kiss—and so much more—in the rain.

Marcus would *never* call himself a romantic, and maybe in all the conventional ways he wasn't. But just the fact that he wanted me to live every experience I never thought I'd have a chance to experience was so touching that it didn't matter if he was generally pragmatic. It made his thoughtfulness special and sweet to me.

I bent forward and put our empty bowl on the coffee table. I'd take it to the kitchen before I went to bed.

"I have to leave tomorrow," he said unexpectedly, his voice decidedly unhappy as he wrapped his arms around me again, and I rested back against him.

It wasn't like I hadn't known his departure was inevitable, but it still stung...hard. "Where do you have to go?" I asked lightly, trying not to sound like the world was ending because it was time for us to part ways.

"I have to go to the Middle East. I wish I could put it off, but—"

"I understand," I interrupted, not wanting to make a big deal out of the fact that he was going. Inside, I was brokenhearted, but I'd known who Marcus was when I'd chosen to spend time with him.

I can't lose it. I've always known this would eventually happen.

I guess I'd just hoped for more time, but honestly, it was going to hurt just as much *whenever* it happened.

"No, you *don't* understand, Danica. I wouldn't leave you right now if I didn't have to," he grumbled.

I suddenly connected something that had happened after we showered. "Does this have anything to do with your conversation with Jett?"

He'd spoken with my brother at length in his office before finally handing the phone over to me when I came downstairs.

He let out a masculine sigh. "That's what's spurring my urgency, yes."

"What happened?" I turned around to look at him in concern.

"It seems we're missing a few virgins," he explained. "Ruby was locked in a room before the auction with two European females, apparently two women who weren't exactly willing participants. Ruby was auctioned off as planned, and as you know, she's safe with your brother in Florida."

"And the other two women?" I questioned.

"They disappeared. They were never part of the auction. Your brother used his skills to track what happened to them. Ruby heard something about them being shipped to Syria, a gift for a rebel leader."

I closed my eyes in horror. "Oh, God. If that's true, they're in trouble, Marcus."

"I know. But I'm hoping they're still over the border in Turkey. Jett found some possible leads."

"Where did he track them to?"

"The same town you left when you decided to follow the teenagers."

It was actually more of a village, and over the years I'd come to know a lot of the locals, and they trusted me. There was often press there, and the town housed a lot of refugees. My job as a journalist had been to report information on the refugee crisis and the status of the fighting in Syria. I knew that area in a personal way. The region also had medical staff from around the world volunteering to help treat the people who had fled to the border town to escape the fighting.

"I'll go with you," I decided. "I know you have more experience with spying than I do, but I know those locals. I speak Turkish and enough Arabic. I can help you get more information if somebody is hiding them."

"Not happening," Marcus answered flatly. "You need more time. You don't want to go back there right now."

"I do," I told him fervently. "I need to go."

Being back in the place that I associated with so much pain was integral to my recovery. I'd always known I had to go eventually. I'd wanted to conquer my fear, but I hadn't gotten to the point where I was ready to return. Now that there were women in trouble, I was ready.

"You're not going, Danica," Marcus insisted. "*Christ!* You just got out of a bad situation. Now you're ready to go risk your neck again?"

"Yes," I said emphatically, my eyes clashing with his in a battle of wills. "Marcus, this is something I *have* to do. I've always known I couldn't let what happened get the best of me. I can't let them win."

"The terrorists who held you captive are dead."

"Not to me," I explained. "I have to face that fear before it will go away. That town had nothing to do with what happened to me, but I connect it in my mind with the pain and fear of my capture and torture."

"Which is exactly why you're not going."

"That's why I *should* go. You'll be there with me, and I can help you."

"I can't do that," he answered in a voice cracking with emotion.

I could see the worry in his expression as I replied, "I'll be safe with you."

"I'd handcuff us together to keep you from running over the border if you think somebody is in trouble."

"I'm good with that," I replied, trying to cajole him into taking me.

"No."

God, he was stubborn. I knew he was trying to protect me from pain, but I couldn't be afraid forever. The thought of going with

Marcus wasn't nearly as scary as going alone. "I won't be afraid. I'll be with you."

"*I'll* be fucking scared," he admitted with a growl. "You've been through enough, Dani."

"I have to go sometime, Marcus. And if I can help you, it's a perfect time. I'm not going to let those bastards win. I'm not spending my life being terrified of a region I spent plenty of my life reporting on. I lived with those people. I was there more than I was here."

"And it was *never* safe," he rumbled. "It's too damn close to the border. The towns in that region *aren't* always secure."

"Is anywhere safe anymore?" I asked. "Anything can happen anywhere in the world."

"I suppose," he conceded. "However, you don't have to put yourself that close to the line of fire."

"I'll go eventually. You can't protect me forever. I'm safer *with* you than *without* you," I reasoned.

I couldn't give in this time. I didn't want to hurt Marcus, but I really needed to go with him and do what I could for the women who hadn't been rescued from Gregory Becker's human trafficking ring. Just the thought of kidnapped women being in the clutches of an evil man like the rebel leader made me nauseous. I knew what they'd suffer, and I knew that they would most likely die after they'd been used like they were an old possession rather than a human being.

"Be ready early," he finally said irritably. "You don't make a move without telling me you're doing it."

My heart clenched as I watched a pained expression cross his face. It was killing him to agree, but I was guessing he decided he would do better with me than without me. He might have contacts in that area, but it wasn't a town he'd spent a ton of time visiting. His appearances had been quick, probably just long enough to meet with his informants in the region.

I lifted my hand and ran it over his lightly whiskered jaw. "Thank you," I said sincerely.

His arms tightened around me. "Hell, I never really had any choice. I knew you'd move your ass like it was on fire once you heard that two women were in trouble."

I smiled. "You're moving pretty quickly yourself."

He shrugged. "Your brother can't go. He's watching out for Ruby."

Maybe he didn't want to make a big deal out of his humanitarian efforts, but Marcus was the type of man who wouldn't be able to live with the fact that he hadn't tried to help those women. "You want to help them, too," I accused gently.

"I *want* to keep your beautiful ass safe. I shouldn't have mentioned the captive women. I should have known you'd jump right into the fire to save them," he countered.

I kissed him tenderly and then pulled back to tell him, "You're a good man, Marcus."

He snorted. "Never heard *that* one before."

"You should. It's true."

"Then you're probably one of the only people who believe that. Most people think I'm an asshole, even my friends."

I laughed at his self-deprecating comment. I'd heard Jett call Marcus a jerk on more than one occasion, but I knew he'd been joking. Underneath his bluster, Marcus was an incredible man. Oh, he was cautious, a trait that probably came from the work he did for the government. But anybody who got to know him would eventually see that underneath the asshole exterior, there was a guy with a very good heart.

"You're taking me with you," I reminded him.

"Reluctantly," he answered in an unhappy tone. "And only because I think you'd get yourself into more trouble without me."

"You know I have more pull in that area," I argued.

"Maybe you do, but I'm still not happy about this entire situation. But I wasn't going to lie to you. I guess I assumed you'd be okay with letting me go alone since it isn't a place you really want to go right now."

"I *need* to go," I said. "I have to set myself free."

"And I want to lock you up," he said huskily.

"We could try out those handcuffs in advance," I suggested.

"You think I won't?" he asked, one arrogant eyebrow raised in challenge.

I wrapped my arms around his neck. "I'm so *not* scared."

In fact, the thought of being naked and at Marcus's mercy was an erotic pleasure I was pretty sure I'd thoroughly enjoy.

He stood, surging to his feet and pulling me up with him. I squealed as he tossed me over his shoulder. "Marcus, let me down. I think you have a fetish about carrying me around like a caveman."

I was laughing as he smacked me on the ass, not listening to a word I said as he made for the bedroom.

"Not a fetish," he denied. "I'm just eager to see you in handcuffs."

I was still smiling as he took me into the bedroom and then set me back on my feet.

"You're impossible," I accused, unable to stop the silly grin from remaining on my face.

"You like that about me," he said arrogantly.

I couldn't argue. He was right. I did, in fact, love his stubbornness when he wasn't driving me crazy.

"I don't love it," I denied falsely, putting my hands on my hips as I rolled my eyes.

"Yeah, you do," he corrected in a husky tone. "You love the way I keep trying until I get you naked, and then *insist* that you come."

Oh, hell. I *did* love that.

"Are you going to keep talking, or are you going to show me?" My body was already on fire for him, and he hadn't even touched me.

He went silent as he got to work on showing me just how much I loved his persistence.

Chapter 25

Marcus

"What the fuck do you mean that they aren't here?" I exploded at Jett, who was on the other end of my cell phone conversation.

We'd only been in Turkey for a day, but it was so fucking hot that I was practically melting in my custom suit and tie.

I was standing at the side of a small street in town, and I'd stopped to call Jett while Dani was just up the road and around the corner talking to one of the locals.

"I mean we found them," Jett answered, seemingly unaffected by my temper. "They were released with the help of a couple of doctors in the same town you're in right now. They made it back to Europe shaken up, but they were okay."

"And you couldn't have found that out before I left US soil with your sister?" I complained, knowing full well it wasn't really Jett's fault.

"Hell, I didn't know you'd take Dani with you."

"Could I stop her?" I drawled.

Danica was capable of bowling people over like a hurricane.

"You probably could have, but you obviously didn't want to," Jett observed.

"Nobody stops Dani when she's determined to do something," I answered in a grim voice.

"She's stubborn," Jett agreed. "*You* should be able to relate to *that*."

"She makes me crazy," I confided. "It's like she's determined to get herself into bad situations."

"She's with you," Jett said. "She'll be okay. And in my sister's defense, she doesn't intentionally try to get in tricky situations. It happens because she cares too damn much. How is she doing mentally?"

"I think she was apprehensive when we first got here. But an hour later, she was running around, talking to the locals and the medical staff here. She seems comfortable here now."

"You care about her," Jett said without question.

"More than I should," I answered reluctantly. "She'll put me through hell."

"She's a handful, but I think you can deal with that because she's also one of the kindest people I know. And I'm not just saying that because she's my sister. Her heart is always in everything she does," Jett threw back at me.

"I know," I admitted. "But sometimes she takes on too many burdens that aren't her own."

"Dani considers anything that she can possibly resolve as her own personal battle. She's always been that way, Marcus. There's nothing any of us can do to change her nature, and I'm not sure I'd want to if I could."

"I know," I told him. "I don't want to change her, but I fucking worry about her."

"Break her heart and I'll kill you," Jett mentioned casually.

"She's more likely to break mine," I mumbled.

"Better yours than hers," Jett said solemnly. "Dani has been through enough. I don't know how you feel about her, but if it isn't something permanent, don't screw with her head."

"Fuck! I *want* it to be permanent. I'm not sure that she wants something that means a commitment." The last thing I wanted to do was scare her away by confessing that I wanted her to stay with me for the rest of our lives. Now that we'd been together, I couldn't imagine spending my life without her. Every second I spent with her was like a gift, and I didn't want it to end.

"If she's with you, she wants something permanent," Jett informed me. "She's not the type to go into anything without wanting everything."

"She's had other men in her life," I argued.

"Not very many," Jett said. "And they were never anything serious."

"What makes you think she wants more than a fling?" I asked curiously.

"Because she's Dani," he said simply. "I've never seen her look at any guy the way she looks at you."

A kernel of hope started to open in my heart. "I hope you're right," I shot back at him. "Otherwise, I'm fucked."

I heard Jett's amused laugh coming from the phone. "Dude, I never thought I'd say this to you, but you're pathetic."

"I know," I agreed readily. "I fucking hate it."

"She's worth it," he argued.

I knew Jett was right. Dani was worth whatever insecurity and fear I had to live through to keep her. Uncomfortable discussing Dani with her brother, I finally asked, "Is everything okay there?"

"Yeah. We're good. Ruby's been through hell, but she's a fighter."

"And you're absolutely certain that those two women are safe?" I asked, wanting to make sure before I told Dani.

"I'm positive," Jett said emphatically. "I just talked to both of them myself. I wish I would have gotten that information before you flew all the way there."

"It's okay," I told him, feeling a little guilty about the way I'd taken his head off verbally. "As you said, you had no idea they were safe a day or two ago. I'm just glad all is well. I can get your sister and get the hell out of here."

"How safe is it there, really?" Jett asked, his voice demanding the truth.

"As safe as it can be for a town near the border, I guess," I told him. "And not nearly as secure as I'd like it. Your sister likes to point out that anything can happen anywhere, but I sure as hell don't like her here. I don't know how I ever left her when I saw her in dangerous areas before."

"Maybe you were in denial," Jett suggested. "I think all of us were. Dani never seemed to be concerned, so all of her siblings, including me, just lived with it. We worried about her, but the longer time went by without anything happening to her, the less anxious we were for her. That was a mistake that will never happen again."

"I fucking worried," I admitted. "But we barely knew each other, and all we did was antagonize each other. I think that's how I dealt with the fear that something would happen to her. If all she did was piss me off, I told myself I was happy to leave her to her own business."

"But it wasn't that simple?" Jett queried.

"*Nothing* with your sister is *ever* that simple," I grumbled. "She still pisses me off."

"But you *still* love her," Jett stated.

More than you'll ever fucking know! Aloud, I answered, "Yeah. Go figure that one out."

"I think anybody you care about, and is worth fighting for, is going to irritate the hell out of you sometimes," Jett replied in a humorous tone.

"I think her stubbornness is one of the things I actually like about her, too, so it's rather paradoxical. Love doesn't make sense," I told Jett in an annoyed voice.

Jett chuckled. "It doesn't *have* to make sense. It wouldn't be so amazing if it did."

I wondered how my friend could still find being in love so attractive since he'd been dumped by an evil bitch who didn't like the way he looked after his accident. I had to give the guy some credit. He'd eventually discovered that what he'd had with Lisette had been one-sided and conditional.

Love wasn't completely comfortable for me. It left me way too vulnerable, and I hated that feeling. But I'd rather be exposed than let go of Danica.

"I guess," I finally answered. "Right now I'm going to find your sister and get the hell out of here so I know she's safe."

"Okay. Let me know when you make it back stateside," Jett requested.

I agreed, and then we both hung up.

I put my phone back in to my jacket pocket. After it was secure, I shrugged out of my suit coat. It was so damn hot that I was sweating bullets.

I undid my tie and pulled that off, too, shoving it into my coat pocket as well.

Although this country had some more temperate areas, this particular town wasn't one of those places, and it was fucking July. It wasn't like Saudi Arabia during the day, but it also lacked any buildings with air conditioning, so the heat was getting incredibly uncomfortable.

I wondered how Dani was faring with her redheaded complexion.

Determined to find her and give her the news that the two women we were searching for were actually safe, I turned and started making my way down the rough street.

We'd ventured into a part of the village that didn't have many people milling around. Her contact had been farther away from the center of town, which was one reason why I'd let her go ahead of me while I checked in with her brother. The area was fairly quiet, so I'd thought it was safe enough to let her out of my direct line of sight. But only just barely. In reality, I'd be able to see her if it wasn't for the buildings.

I was almost to the corner when the blast occurred. Later, I'd never remember seeing the young, inexperienced suicide bomber who came into town behind me.

All I'd remember was the way the bomb had exploded like everything in the area was going up in smoke.

Shattering glass.

The force of the explosion knocking me down into the dirt, my head connecting with the street.

For a few moments, I knew nothing.

After that, all I experienced was fear in the debris-filled air as I saw the shop around the corner that Dani had gone to visit, and my determination to get Dani out of the collapsing building even if I had to claw my way in.

Chapter 26

Dani

The explosion had taken me completely by surprise, so I'd never quite understood what hit me.

Stunned, I was on the dirt floor, still trying to process what had happened when my mind latched on to one thing: Marcus was outside.

Marcus. Oh, God. Was he safe?

"A bomb. It had to be a bomb," I muttered to myself. "And it was close."

I wasn't unfamiliar with the sound of a bomb exploding, but it had taken a minute to shake off the shock and realize exactly what had happened so close to my location. I'd never experienced the noise quite so loud or so devastating.

The entire building had come down on top of my head. I had a small space to move, but there was no way I could get myself out of the debris. Part of the ceiling was right above me, and between the rafters on the ground, I could see a ton of broken glass.

If I'm in a desperate situation like this…how is Marcus?

He'd been out in the open, exposed to the full force of the explosives.

My eyes were starting to adjust to the dim atmosphere around me, the air still loaded with small particles and smoke.

"Baris!" I tried to call out to my friend who had been across the room from me when the bomb had gone off.

He didn't answer, and I was hoping he had gotten clear of the falling building. Baris had been close to the exit, so it was entirely possible he was safe.

I kept shouting out my friend's name, but there was no response.

There were voices outside screaming, so help had arrived, but my heart was pounding as I laid my aching head down on the dirt.

"Please let Marcus be okay," I murmured in a painful whisper. "Don't let anything happen to him."

A tear trickled down my cheek, my heart desperately wanting to deny that he could be injured...or worse.

"I love him," I said aloud, hearing the words I'd been keeping inside my mind for days.

It was a relief to admit to myself exactly how I felt about Marcus. Honestly, I'd probably always just been a little bit in love with the frustrating alpha male. But it had really grown during the time we'd spent together in Florida and in Colorado. I'd gotten to know who Marcus was inside, and fallen completely, head-over-heels in love for the very first time in my life.

It felt good.

But it also hurt because I knew our relationship would be temporary.

Marcus would eventually have to go back to traveling, and I'd move on to my next story. Problem was, I hadn't wanted to miss a moment of what was in between those events, so I'd let myself experience the pleasure. I'd pay a high price for indulging, but it didn't matter.

He'd probably been the only man I could have trusted enough to sleep with after what had happened to me.

It was ironic that the very healing I'd experienced with Marcus would probably break my heart in the future.

"Just let him be okay. I'll deal with everything else when the time comes," I whispered, my throat too sore now to speak louder. The smoke and dust was getting to me.

I tormented myself about Marcus's safety, trapped until somebody came along to help me out of the toppled building. I felt so damn guilty. I'd been the one to get Marcus into this position. If he hadn't come to Florida to find me, he probably wouldn't be in this particular border town right now. If not for me, he'd be safe.

I told myself over and over that I couldn't think about the past, but I still did. If something happened to Marcus, I'd hate myself for insisting that I go with him. Even if he'd still ended up here looking for the missing women, he definitely wouldn't have been in this area. It was me who had brought him here because I had my own contacts to see.

"Please be okay. Please be okay."

I chanted the words under my breath, the small phrase becoming my mantra.

I'd come here to help save lives, and I'd quickly regained my confidence and lost my fear of this town and the surrounding area. It hadn't taken me long after I'd arrived here to get back into the swing of hunting down information. The friends I'd made in this village had greeted me warmly, all of them happy that I was doing okay.

Finally, I'd felt like I was making a recovery from my fears.

I just desperately hoped that I hadn't gotten Marcus hurt in the process.

If it wasn't for me, he most likely wouldn't have been in Turkey right now, much less a border town that evidently had just taken some kind of bomb strike.

He never would have gotten involved in Miami if I hadn't been chasing after Becker, and it would have been a much lengthier time until we'd run into each other again.

I closed my eyes, the smoke and dirty air around me starting to make them burn like crazy.

Even though I loved Marcus more than anything, I'd give everything up right now just to see him be safe.

I have to find him!

I really wanted to get the hell out of this store and go find Marcus, but if I started to move, I'd more than likely cause the roof to come down on top of me. I needed somebody to move stuff from the outside in so I had an escape route without moving some of the supports around me that were keeping me from getting crushed.

My heart started to hammer as I heard movement coming from outside the building. I could hear people working on digging me out. Although I had no patience for waiting, I had to keep myself alive so I could do everything I could to help Marcus. I had to find him, and to accomplish that, I'd have to get out of this spot alive.

"Danica!"

My heart lurched as I heard a male voice calling my name. A tone that sounded very much like Marcus.

My eyes popped open, and I could see someone progressively making their way to my location, the masculine figure tossing large pieces of debris aside much faster than he ought to be able to move.

"Marcus!" I shrieked.

"Dani?" he called, his voice hoarse and stressed out.

"I'm here. Be careful. The roof is going to collapse. There isn't much holding it above the ground."

I could see him now, and I watched as he pushed away the loose wood, being careful that he didn't yank out a necessary piece.

"Are you okay?" he hollered.

"Yes. I just need an opening to get out. If I move some of these pieces near me to get out of here, I'm afraid the roof will go."

"Don't fucking move," Marcus demanded. "I'll clear a path from here."

"Are you okay?" I asked anxiously.

"Hell, no, I'm *not* okay. I'm goddamn terrified that you're going to get crushed."

It was a typical *Marcus* kind of reply, but so incredibly sweet that it made my tears flow steadily. "I meant are you *physically* all right? Were you hurt in the explosion?"

"I'll live," he said in a voice loud enough to travel.

To me, that meant that he was injured, but didn't want to admit it.

I finally saw his face as he crouched at the end of an opening he'd cleared with his bare hands.

"Marcus, you are hurt," I cried out, anxious because I could see the blood on his face.

"I'm fine," he said sharply. "Right now all I want is to get you out of here. Can you give me your hands without upsetting anything? I'll pull you out through the area I just cleared."

He was downplaying his injuries, but I wasn't going to get any answers until I got away from the building.

"Yes. I can move them." I lifted my arms carefully, stretching out so I could clasp his hands.

"Are you hurt? I don't want to make anything worse," he questioned hesitantly.

"No," I replied. "I was confused for a few minutes, but I'm not hurt."

He reached into my space, grasping my hands and then pulled me out, slow and steady. I carefully tried to keep myself positioned away from the beams that I was fairly certain was keeping the roof from hitting the ground.

In just a few moments, I was out, away from the building, and being held tightly in Marcus's arms.

We clung to each other, and I never wanted to let him go. In the moments I'd questioned whether or not he was still alive, I'd nearly died myself.

"Baris?" I asked anxiously about my friend as I hugged Marcus just as firmly as he was holding me.

"He's okay," Marcus answered. "Just a few minor injuries. He's being treated at the clinic."

I pulled back so I could look at him.

I reached up to touch the gash on his head. I couldn't help but notice his hands were also bleeding from digging through the wood and glass to get me out of my prison barehanded. "You're hurt, Marcus. You need to get to the medical clinic."

The wound on his head was open and blood was still flowing from his injury. The shirt that had been white this morning was now covered in his blood. No doubt the head wound had just kept on bleeding as he'd pulled me out of the wreckage of the store.

"I'm good," he said in a tone heavy with emotion. "I just want to get you the hell out of here."

"I'm okay," I argued.

"I'm not," he confessed. "I don't ever want to live through another incident of not knowing whether you're dead or alive, Danica. I can't."

"I was scared, too," I said in a tremulous voice as I put my arms around him again and hugged him to me. "I knew you were outside. I didn't know where you were when the bomb exploded."

"I was worrying about you. It seems I'm rather good at doing that now," he answered, his torn-up hands stroking over my hair in a comforting motion.

"We're safe," I said tearfully, the enormity of what had just happened starting to sink in.

"Let's go home," he suggested, but he didn't move.

"We have to find those women—"

"They're safe," Marcus told me. "Somebody helped them get home. Jett confirmed it."

Oh, God. The irony didn't escape me that we were in Turkey looking for the two women, and they were home safe. We'd nearly gotten ourselves killed for two females who hadn't needed our help.

Even though it hurt to separate myself from Marcus, I pulled back so we could leave. "You need to have your injuries checked before we go," I insisted, concerned about the size of the laceration on his head.

"I'll have them checked when we get home," he said stubbornly.

"Now," I demanded.

I expected a smart-ass answer, and I was actually concerned when I didn't get it. I looked at Marcus anxiously, noting that he was pale, and he was holding his hand to his head.

"I'll be..." His voice trailed off as he sat down on a nearby crate that hadn't been blown away.

I squatted beside him. "Marcus, talk to me," I said in a panic.

He never said another word.

He lost consciousness as I struggled to hold him up, screaming for somebody—anybody—to help me.

Chapter 27

Dani

Two days later, we were finally on board Marcus's jet, headed for home.

He'd scared the hell out of me, and I'd never let him forget it. After he'd been treated as much as he could be at the medical clinic, he'd been transported to the capital city for further testing. He'd stayed a few days there for observation after the tests had come out negative for fractures. Marcus had one hell of a concussion, but he was recovering.

Luckily, the suicide bomber had been inexperienced. Just a girl, really, somewhere around the age of eighteen. Alone, she'd wandered into the wrong part of the town, and there had been plenty of damage, but no fatalities except for the rebel bomber.

I mourned the life of somebody that young, and I'd felt a profound sadness that she'd been so full of violence.

"Hey, are you okay?" Marcus asked from his supine position on the bed. We'd lifted off and then I'd insisted on bringing him back to rest.

I was sitting cross-legged next to him, lost in my thoughts as I looked at the bandage on his forehead. I'd lost count of the number of sutures it had taken to close his laceration, but it was healing well. "Just tired, I guess," I answered as I smiled down at him.

"You *are* in a bed now," he reminded me.

I rubbed a hand over my eyes. "I know. But I've had a hard time sleeping."

"Worried about me?" he asked curiously.

I gave him an exasperated look. "Yes, I was worried."

"I have a pretty hard head," he said in an amused tone, his hand stroking over my back with a soothing touch.

His palms and fingers were already healing. Luckily, the damage to his hands had been superficial.

I snorted. "For once, I'm *glad* you're hard-headed."

I maneuvered my body down so I could lie next to him on my side, my head propped up on my hand.

"I'm doing all right. So why the pensive look on your face?" he asked in a tender voice.

Gently, I reached up to stroke the hair from his forehead. "I just keep thinking how things could have worked out. If you'd been closer, it could have been really bad."

"Don't, Dani," he said sternly. "Don't drive yourself crazy with how ugly it could have been. I tortured myself with the same thoughts for the first day after it happened. Then I realized how damn lucky we are. I'm focusing on the fact that we're both still here, and relatively unscathed."

Marcus could make light of his injuries, but I couldn't. Otherwise, he was right. I really needed to be glad we were both still alive. He would heal, and be back to normal in a week or so. Except for maybe a small scar, he wouldn't have any lasting effects from the explosion.

"I know you're right, but I was really scared," I confided.

Marcus wrapped an arm around my waist and pulled me against his body. I relaxed, letting my head drop onto his chest.

"You asked me once what I was afraid of," Marcus said thoughtfully.

"I remember," I muttered.

"What happened is exactly what I'm fucking terrified about," he said in a graveled voice. "I'm scared as hell that something will happen to you. You don't exactly live a noneventful life, and that worries me. I don't get uptight about very many things, but losing you or seeing you hurt again is my greatest fear. I can't see you brutalized and broken again, Dani. It almost killed me after we pulled you out of that rebel camp."

My eyes teared up, and no matter how hard I tried to blink them back, they still fell. "But I survived, Marcus. Maybe I'll never be quite the same as I was before it happened, but I realized even before the bombing that going back had somehow set me free."

He was silent for a moment before he asked, "Do you mean that?"

"Yes. I'm not saying that I don't need to keep meeting with my counselor, but I think everything fell into place, all I need to do now is sort it all out. I'm not anxious anymore. I doubt I'll ever be as fearless as I used to be. But some of that lack of fear was based on the fact that I'd never really understood how quickly life could end. I'd never really experienced intense pain or fear. After I did, I was warier."

"I never want to see you afraid, in pain, or anxious," he grumbled.

"I don't welcome it, either," I admitted. "But I have to admit that no matter how much I'd like to go back and be the same person I was before the kidnapping, I can't. I have to be okay with who I am now."

"Are you?"

"Yeah. I think I am," I mused.

"Did going back make you want to get your old life back?" he asked hesitantly.

I sighed. "No. I can never go back. I have to move forward. I'd like to stay a freelance investigative reporter wherever there are stories to be told. But I'm not sad I gave up my beat anymore. I've discovered that I don't always have to be in every hot spot in the world. I can find my stories that need to be told in all parts of the world."

"Thank fuck," Marcus cursed. "I want you to be with me."

I tried to ignore the way my heart was galloping inside my chest. I loved Marcus with every fiber of my being, but I wasn't going to get my hopes up that our time wasn't going to be limited. "You'll go back to traveling eventually," I said lightly, trying to pretend that separating wouldn't tear my heart out.

"Not as much," he informed me. "It seems my executives are doing my job quite well overseas, and if the government doesn't have a problem with me training somebody to do some of my intel work, I think I have the perfect man to take over."

"You're going to stop being James Bond?" I asked incredulously.

"I'm *not* playing James Bond, and yes, I don't think I'd mind turning some of that over to somebody younger. I'm tired of not eating chocolate," he teased. "It's not that I won't travel, and I'll still meet up with some of my contacts for intel, but I'm about ready to spend more time with my family and at my home in Rocky Springs. I regret that I've missed so much because I'm constantly away."

I understood how alone a person could feel when they were traveling all the time. I'd felt separated from my siblings for a long time, and I missed them. "I missed my family, too," I confessed. "I think I just kept myself too busy to notice."

"You never commented on what I said," he reminded me.

"What?"

"I want you to be with me, Dani. I want you to stay with me. Will you?" His voice was hopeful.

"I don't know if I can," I replied honestly, tears still pouring from my eyes and landing on the bare skin of his chest.

"Why?" he grunted.

I was quiet, afraid to tell him about everything I was thinking. I didn't want him to feel pressured for more, but I had to be true to myself. "I love you, Marcus."

He rolled onto his side and propped his head up, forcing me to do the same, so we were facing each other. "What did you say?"

"You heard me. I love you so much it hurts. I'm not sure I can be in a relationship with you and not want more than just sex."

"You and I have *never* been all about sex," he protested. "Jesus, Dani! Can't you feel it? I think I've known that we were more than just sexually attracted for a long time, but I didn't want to acknowledge it. Yeah. Okay. My primary instinct was to fuck you, and that's never gone away. But I think we both know this has never completely been about sex."

"I didn't think so, but I wasn't sure what you wanted. I didn't know if you wanted love, but I can't *not* say it anymore."

"I fucking want it all," he said in a warning voice. "I want everything you're willing to give, and then I'll want more after that."

"You want something that involves a commitment?"

"Oh, hell, yeah. I want you and I to be as committed as two people can get," he answered in a husky voice. "I want to hammer out some kind of compromise so we can travel together, and be home at the same damn time. I want you to marry me, and wear my ring on your finger so every bastard out there knows that you're mine."

"You want me to marry you?" I asked apprehensively.

Marcus Colter wasn't a marrying type of guy...or I'd never seen him as one until now.

"I can't believe you would ever doubt that I wanted us to be together. I love you, too, Danica. Say you'll marry me so I don't have to have a heart attack over whether or not you're going to agree."

My eyes met his in a clash of intensity that was flowing between the two of us.

Maybe I'd always had doubts about where we could go as a couple, but now that I knew he loved me, too, I felt like I could fly. "Yes," I answered simply.

"Yes, you will?" Marcus probed. "Will you marry me? I don't have a ring yet, but—"

I put a gentle hand in his hair and cut off his words as I leaned forward to kiss him. I didn't give a damn about a ring, or the formalities. All I needed to know was that he loved me.

Everything else was nothing more than inconsequential details.

He wrapped an arm around my waist and then pushed me onto my back, his mouth demanding as he took control of the embrace.

It was the sweetest, hottest kiss I'd ever experienced.

He lingered, nipping at my bottom lip, and then soothing it with his tongue.

The kiss wasn't carnal, and I wasn't about to let it get out of control. It wasn't going anywhere. Marcus was fresh out of the hospital. The last thing he needed right now was bedroom Olympics.

But we could savor the moment, and all of the emotions that went along with deciding that we loved each other so much that we wanted to spend the rest of our lives together.

When he finally lifted his head, I looked into his eyes and simply said, "Yes. I'll marry you. I'll stay with you. I'll continue to let you steal my chocolate for as long as we both shall live," I joked. "Now you need to get some rest."

"I'd rather get you naked," he answered.

"No sex. We both just admitted this isn't all about sex. And you just got out of the hospital. No strenuous activities for you."

His expression was disappointed. "I know it's not *all* sexual, but that doesn't mean I still don't desperately want you naked."

I wanted him, too, but I was content to wait. "Your health is my biggest priority."

"Mine, too," he said in a grim voice. "My balls are blue right now."

I laughed out loud. I couldn't believe he actually wanted to have sex when he was still recovering from his injuries. "Go to sleep," I insisted, pushing him onto his back. "The last thing you need to think about right now is getting laid."

"It's the first thing I'm thinking about," he answered glumly.

"You can go a few days without," I told him as I settled beside him and put my head on his chest.

"Yeah, I can," he admitted. "Hell, I used to go without for months, or even a year. But since the first time I touched you in Florida, I can't fucking think about anything else."

I smiled against the smooth skin of his chest. Honestly, I pretty much felt the same way, but I wasn't going to admit it right now. "I love you, Marcus," I murmured instead.

"Christ! I love you, too, baby," he said in a husky voice as he wrapped his arms tightly around me. "You can check one more thing off your bucket list because you're never going to find a guy who loves you as much as I do."

I sighed, happy as I heard Marcus's breathing even out, a definite sign that he was exhausted and needed to rest.

He wants to spend the rest of our lives together. He wants to marry me.

I decided it was finally time for me to close the window of my past and throw open the door to my future with Marcus.

A tear trickled down my cheek, but it wasn't from sadness or fear. It was created from the intense joy that was in my heart, and the knowledge that Marcus loved me as much as I loved him.

All of the pain I'd gone through was over, and I was finally ready to move on.

Knowing that I was sprinting forward with a man I loved more than life itself made my new mindset that much sweeter than it ever had been before.

He was the important piece of the puzzle of my life that had always been missing, even though I'd never known it until he had been fit snugly into that empty space.

I fell into an exhausted sleep, held safely in his arms, knowing that no matter how irritated I made him, and vice versa, there would *always* be love.

Chapter 28

Dani

"I love how close all of your family is with each other," I told Marcus a few days later as we drove home from dinner at his mother's house in Rocky Springs.

It was a beautifully clear summer's evening. Because we were riding in one of Marcus's many sports cars, I could see the stars. The convertible gave me a perfect view of the Colorado sky.

I relished the feel of being in the open air. My hair would probably end up looking like a bird's nest, but to feel this way, so free and buoyant, it was completely worth it.

"Your family is close," he replied.

I shrugged. "When we're all able to get together. I think so much fell apart when my parents died so suddenly. We all sort of went our own way to deal with our grief. Your mom seems to hold everything together in your family."

"I agree," he answered. "She's been the glue that's fused our family together since my father died. But traveling the world doesn't help. We both have some time to try to make up with our families."

Marcus and I had talked a lot about what we wanted to do in the future.

I would see a lot more of Harper since we were in the same town, and my sister and I had vowed to try to get together more with our brothers. Harper would still be traveling with her senator husband, Blake, back and forth to Washington, DC, and I wanted to travel with Marcus internationally so I could find my own stories to write. But Harper and I would both be home and in one place a lot more often, so we were determined to force ourselves into our brothers' lives if necessary.

I loved every one of my siblings. None of us had ever wanted to grow apart.

It had just...happened.

Marcus reached out for my hand, and I entwined my fingers with his as I finally promised, "We'll make time in the future."

I already adored Tate, and his wife, Lara. Zane and his wife, Ellie, were both extremely kind. I'd met Gabe and Chloe for the first time earlier in the evening. And of course, Harper and Blake had been at the family supper, too.

Honestly, I already knew that I was going to come to love Marcus's family as much as he did. The Colter women were already trying to pull me into their circle by planning various activities together. It was going to be nice to have family again, but having Marcus's family wouldn't lessen my efforts with Harper to pull my brothers Jett, Carter, and Mason back into the fold.

I smiled as we pulled into Marcus's driveway and he took the small paved road that drove around the massive house and to the back where he had a ten-car garage where he stored his *summer* cars. There was a three-car garage attached to the house where he kept his luxury vehicles that were appropriate for all-weather driving.

As serious and sensible as Marcus was, I was delighted to see that he was still a boy who loved his toys. All ten spaces were full of luxury or classic sports cars. It seemed to be Marcus's one big indulgence, and I wasn't about to complain. He could afford them, and I got the benefit of riding in the powerhouse vehicles.

Eventually, I'd finagle him into letting me drive all of them. A girl loved her toys, too.

After he closed up the garage, he took my hand and we walked to the house together. "It seems strange to actually have a permanent home," I said in a thoughtful voice.

I'd spent years running all over the planet, but I'd never invested in a home. Yeah, Harper and I had purchased the condo in Miami together, but that was more of an investment than a home.

"If you don't like this one, we can buy a different house," he suggested.

Oh, hell no. "You had this home built custom," I scolded. "And I love it."

Marcus's house was enormous, but it was a reflection of him, and I couldn't have planned out a better home for us.

He let me into the house and disabled the alarm before he turned back to me. "I don't want this to be all about me, Dani. Hell, I don't even know if you want to live in Rocky Springs. I can live anywhere, but I can't live without you."

I threw myself into his arms, my heart so light it nearly floated out of my chest. "It's *not* all about you. I don't have a home, Marcus. I never bothered because I was too busy trying to chase stories. But this is where we both grew up, and my sister is here. It's perfect."

His arms tightened around my waist. "I just want you to be happy," he grumbled.

I pulled back so I could look up at his face. "Tell me you love me," I requested.

His beautiful silver eyes were flashing fire as he said obligingly, "I love you."

I ran a hand along the dark stubble on his jaw. "That's all I need to be ecstatically happy."

He nodded and shot me a wicked grin that immediately had heat pooling between my thighs.

When Marcus smiled, my world turned upside down.

He clasped my hand and pulled me toward the kitchen. "I'm glad you feel that way, love, because there's more."

Bemused, I followed his lead. I wasn't sure how much more *happiness* I could handle.

I stopped abruptly as we entered the kitchen. "What in the world…"

The kitchen table was full of items, but the first thing that caught my attention was two heart-shaped balloons attached to the most beautiful bouquet of red roses I'd ever seen.

One balloon said "Marry."

The second said "Me."

I covered my mouth, my emotions close to the surface. "I already said *yes*," I reminded him in a tearful tone. "How did you do this?"

"I do have assistants," he said. "You just haven't met them yet. I had to enlist some help to get this stuff here while we were gone."

I gently ran a finger over the roses, and then noticed that nearly the entire table was filled with chocolate.

"You have good taste," I said in an amused voice. I recognized most of the names on the boxes and wrappings. Everything on the table was the best of the best in chocolate, and pricey as hell. He'd gotten everything from master chocolatiers from Switzerland to France, and one from the East Coast of the US.

More often than not, I'd settled for a candy bar from a convenience store. I wasn't that picky about how I got my chocolate. But I wasn't averse to trying some of the items Marcus had gotten. In fact, I was downright eager to tear into the collection.

He stepped up to the table and drew a bottle of fine champagne from its icy confinement, and then uncorked it and poured it into a beautiful pair of crystal flutes.

I accepted the one he handed me, my heart racing at the thought of how much trouble Marcus had gone to just to please me. "Thank you," I said in a tremulous voice.

"It's no more than you deserve," Marcus told me as he took a sip of his champagne. "I never should have proposed in the bedroom of my damn jet. You deserve so much more than that. You're my heart, Danica."

I opened my mouth to answer him, to tell him that he was my everything, but I closed it again as I heard a high-pitched bark.

"One more thing..." His voice trailed off as he walked across the large kitchen and bent over to fumble with what looked like a crate of some kind.

I was flummoxed as a bundle of fur exploded from its confinement and hurdled straight toward me. "Oh, my God," I squealed, putting my wine glass on the table so I could catch the small canine body. "Who is this?"

"You did say you always wanted a dog. Technically, this is a puppy, but he will eventually be full-sized," he informed me.

I cuddled the squirming, excited puppy as I asked, "So it's a boy? Is he mine?"

Marcus nodded. "Yours," he confirmed.

I beamed up at him. "I'll share him with you. He looks like a German Shepherd. Does he have a name?"

"Not yet. But he will when you give him one. And he is a German Shepherd. Tate has a male, and he wanted to breed Shep with a female before he got him fixed. This puppy is one of Shep's offspring."

"He's gorgeous," I said emphatically, laughing as the pup left my lap and started bouncing around the room and then ran back to me.

I stared at his collar for a moment before I reached out and tried to grab the shiny object attached to the blue collar.

It took me a moment to understand what I was holding.

"Is this mine, too?"

Marcus moved forward and offered his hand. I took it, allowing him to pull me to my feet. "If you're still willing to accept it and everything that comes along with being married to a guy like me, it's yours."

I fingered the beautiful ring I'd snagged from the puppy's collar, my eyes filled with happy tears. I got entirely choked up as Marcus took the ring, reached for my hand, and slid the incredible diamond on my finger as he added, "If you don't want it, you're too late. You're mine now."

"I want it," I shrieked as he twirled me in the air.

"I'm sorry that I wasn't ready when I proposed," he said huskily. "But you can cross another item off your bucket list. You got a proposal, even if it wasn't all that slick."

He'd just put an absolutely amazing ring on my finger, and he was apologizing? "It doesn't matter."

"It matters," he argued. "I don't want you to ever regret that you married a guy who isn't very romantic."

Maybe Marcus wasn't hearts and flowers every day, but I'd never doubt how much he loved me. This huge display just to propose to a woman who had already said *yes* was a perfect example of why I'd never think he wasn't romantic. "I'd never regret you," I said fiercely. "Never."

His mouth came down on mine so quickly that he took my breath away. I moaned against his lips, my body needy as I opened to him willingly, letting him plunder my mouth.

I was on fire, and I wasn't sure anything could ever extinguish the blaze.

My arms tightened around his neck, I pressed against him, feeling his enlarged cock through the denim of his jeans.

I hadn't crumbled under his other assaults to my senses, willing to wait until he was completely recovered. They'd taken his sutures out earlier today, and I'd had a feeling that I wasn't going to be able to resist our mutual hunger for each other much longer.

"Marcus," I gasped as he lifted his head.

"I know, baby. Hold on," he crooned as he lifted the cotton skirt of my casual sundress, and then stroked his fingers over my saturated panties.

My head fell back as the heat of his touch consumed me. "Yes. Now. Please."

I couldn't wait for him to fuck me after days of self-deprivation. I wanted him inside me, his hips thrusting over and over until we were both spent.

He crunched up the panties in his hand, and then tugged hard. "No more waiting," he said, demanding.

"No more waiting," I repeated as I felt the small piece of torn, silken material slip down my legs and to the floor.

My core clenched ferociously as Marcus stroked through my folds and his fingers entered my wet heat.

I moaned again as he teased my clit, ready to plead for mercy.

His hands finally grasped my ass, and he carried me over to the table and set my butt down on the edge. He cleared space with a wide sweep of his muscular arm, and I never mourned the expensive chocolate that hit the floor.

I craved Marcus so much more than I longed for any kind of chocolate.

I propped myself up on my arms and watched as he furiously freed his cock from his jeans.

"Can't. Wait," he growled. "Put your legs around me."

"Don't wait," I pleaded as I obeyed his command. "Now."

I inhaled sharply as he pulled my body forward and buried himself inside me in one powerful thrust.

"Yes. Just like that. No holding back," I panted.

"I couldn't if I wanted to," he answered in a low, carnal tone.

It was hard and fast. Beautiful and frenzied. Marcus pummeled into me with a desperation that I returned.

"More," I cried.

He gave me more, and then he did it again.

Keeping up his punishing pace, my body started to tremble as Marcus pounded into me with no mercy. All I could do was ride the wave of desire that had flooded me, and then took over my body until all I could think of was the man that seemed eager to drive me completely insane.

He tightened his hold on the cheeks of my ass, holding me in place while he kept stroking into me over and over.

"I need to come, Marcus," I whimpered.

"Then come for me," he replied in a raw, feral tone. He took a hand from my ass, and then found the spot I needed him to touch with his fingers.

"Yes. Yes. Yes." I let go and let the force of my orgasm take control. I rode the climax to a crescendo, my body writhing under his ministrations. My core started to spasm. The muscles in my sheath were trying to milk him dry.

"Marcus. I love you so much," I screamed, my whole being trembling under the force of my powerful release.

"I love you," he returned in a groan of pure relief, surging a few more times as he emptied himself inside me.

I sat up, threw my arms around his neck, and kissed him.

It was a long, leisurely embrace. I speared one hand through the hair at the back of his head, sighing into his mouth as he held me tightly. "Marcus," I said in a whisper as I pulled my head back.

We clung to each other. I wasn't sure how long we stayed in that position, but it took the puppy's annoyed bark to snap us out of our own little world, both of us laughing as we finally pulled our satiated bodies apart.

I picked up my destroyed undies and tossed them into the garbage can without a single ounce of remorse.

I was rich. Marcus was rich. I could buy new panties. But nothing could ever replace what had just happened between us.

Money could never buy this kind of happiness.

I smiled as I watched Marcus give our new puppy the affection it wanted.

If I had the man I loved, I could easily learn to just buy my underwear in mass quantities in the future.

Epilogue

Marcus

Several months later...

"Harper is pregnant," Blake announced without warning in a terrified voice.

My twin and I were hitting a few stores in Rocky Springs before we met up with Harper and Dani for lunch.

Strangely enough, we were at a specialty candy shop, and we were both looking.

I wasn't really surprised that Blake's wife was pregnant since I was pretty sure he practiced at getting her pregnant a lot. He adored his wife, and I knew Blake wanted kids, so I asked, "And this isn't a good thing?"

He picked up a box of chocolates and then put them down again as he replied, "It wasn't supposed to happen. She can't have children, but I knew that when I married her."

"Then how did she get pregnant?"

I was assuming he'd done it in the normal way, but I didn't want to go there with my brother.

"It just happened. I guess it was possible, but highly unlikely. We've talked about adopting. We didn't expect this to happen."

"Congratulations," I said as I clapped him on the back. "But you don't seem happy."

"I'm fucking terrified," Blake confessed. "Everything is normal so far, but anything could happen. She lost a baby after we separated over ten years ago. *My* child. *Our* child."

I knew women gave birth every day, but the whole situation seemed a little frightening to me, too. Hell, I didn't know how I'd be feeling if Dani was pregnant. Someday, I'd probably find out, but I was glad right now that I wasn't in Blake's shoes.

"I'm sorry," I told my twin in a hoarse voice.

I was sad that I'd lost a niece or nephew, and that Blake had lost a child.

"Thanks," he said, his attention drawn away by an oversized candy bar. "I know it's a good thing, but I'm afraid something might happen again."

That sounded like a legitimate concern. "Is the pregnancy high-risk?"

"Not really," he told me. "Everything is going well. I don't want to tell Harper that I'm a wreck. We promised we'd focus on the positive, and she needs that right now."

Blake and I had gotten closer over the last few months, so it wasn't unusual for me to answer, "Then focus on the fact that you're going to have a baby, and try to forget about something you can't control."

Easy for me to say, but I understood what loving someone as much as Blake and I loved our wives could do to a guy. Knowing his wife was pregnant and that she'd previously lost a child was probably eating Blake up inside.

"I'm happy," Blake said in a decidedly *unhappy* voice. "I just wish the pregnancy part was over."

I picked up a box of Dani's favorite candy and held onto it while I followed my brother around the store. "Are you going to buy something?"

Blake startled like I'd just woke him up. "Yeah," he said absently as he picked out a couple of different boxes and we moved toward the register to pay.

"How long until it's over?" I asked curiously as I paid for my purchase.

"Six months, twenty days, and about twelve hours until her due date," Blake said, stepping up to pay for his candy.

Poor bastard. He'll crack. He'll never make it that long.

We wandered toward the café next door after we were finished, neither one of us in a hurry since we were running ahead of schedule.

I didn't have words to make Blake feel better. I knew from experience that his anxiety wasn't going to pass until Harper delivered a healthy baby. "It will be okay," I finally said in a tone that I hoped was some kind of a voice of reason. "If it's not high-risk, the chances are excellent that she'll get through it just fine."

"I know. But I'll be worried until she's delivered," Blake said as he looked at his watch. "What do you think our women are doing?" he questioned.

"Probably in the children's store," I guessed.

Blake suddenly grinned. "Highly likely," he agreed. "Harper is buying things for the baby already."

For a moment, I saw Blake's apprehension dissolve as he became focused on the pleasant parts of having a child.

He looked...happy.

Maybe I hadn't understood his desire to marry before, but now that Dani was my wife, I was living in the same kind of "happiness bubble" as my other brothers and Chloe.

Not that everything was perfect between Dani and I. Putting two hard-headed individuals together for a lifetime meant there were going to be some disagreements, but I'd decided a long time ago that I'd rather fight with her than screw any other female.

Besides, there was always the makeup sex. Now *that* was worth the occasional fight.

Honestly, I knew I was an asshole, and she was still my angel—even when we disagreed. Just the fact that she'd been willing to take my ass on for the rest of her life had been a goddamn miracle.

I'd married her soon after I'd gotten a ring on her finger. Having a family as big as mine all in the same area had helped us say our vows within a few weeks, my mother and the rest of the family doing their share to help Dani and I pull off a nice wedding in record time.

Blake and I were nearly to the restaurant when we were greeted by the sight of our wives coming down the sidewalk toward us.

I watched Dani laugh at something Harper had said, her face lit up by the happiness she'd found here with our families. She was extremely tight with her sister, and had become close to all of the Colter women.

I got together with my brothers on a regular basis. Blake and I were more like twins again, and we'd probably always have that certain affinity with each other now that we were together more often. He traveled back and forth to Washington, DC for his Senate duties, but we saw each other often enough.

"She's so fucking beautiful," I muttered as I watched her and Harper get closer.

"They *both* are," Blake corrected.

Dani was still in counseling, but I knew she was getting more confident and sassy every single day. Not that she hadn't *always* been audacious, but little by little, I saw less and less of the haunted look she'd once had in her eyes.

She was still writing, and she'd even done some special interest pieces in the local newspaper. If something could be argued, my wife would do it with gusto, whether it was a regional issue or relevant to the entire world. Regardless of where she was publishing one of her articles, she put her whole damn heart into every single issue she wrote about.

Dani finally looked up, and our eyes were immediately drawn to each other. Hell, I swore that I had a homing beacon that would always lead me directly to her.

My heart started to accelerate as she smiled at me, beaming with a beautiful bright light that I always associated with her jubilant grin.

Jesus Christ! How did I get lucky enough to get a woman who loves me as much as I love her?

She increased her stride, and I caught her as she careened into my chest. My arms wrapped around her tightly, and of course, my dick responded accordingly. There was no way I could smell her sweet scent without my cock going into the *completely ready* mode.

"I love you," Dani said in a breathless voice as she pulled back and gave me a short, affectionate kiss.

"I love you, too," I answered in a husky voice. I doubted there would ever be a time when I could hear those three little words from her without feeling like I had a ten-pound lump in my throat.

"Harper is going to have a baby," she announced happily. "I'm so excited. We're going to have a niece or nephew."

I shot a grin at Blake and Harper, who had just finished their own intimate greeting. "I heard. Congratulations, Harper."

Harper smiled at me. "Thanks. Now if I could just keep Blake from worrying."

"It will never happen," I told my sister-in-law bluntly.

"Nothing wrong with wishful thinking," Harper replied, placing a kiss on her husband's cheek. "Dani is going to throw me a baby shower."

"Why?" Blake asked, sounding genuinely confused. "I thought those were held just for gifts. We're rich. You can buy whatever you want."

I shook my head. Obviously my twin hadn't quite figured out women yet. "There is usually junk food and cake," I explained. "And it's the perfect opportunity for women to get together and complain about us."

Dani gave me a playful shove. "That's not the *only* reason. Being pregnant is a big deal, and it's a celebration."

Really, for Harper, the pregnancy *was* a miracle, and she had more to celebrate than many other women. I'd been teasing my brother and Dani, but I was really delighted for my brother and Harper.

"Then we'll make it a real party," I agreed happily. "Chocolate cake?"

"Of course," both Dani and Harper answered at the same time.

I grinned at my wife and handed over the bag of chocolate. "Maybe this will tide you over until we can order the cake."

She snatched the bag and held it to her chest. "Oh, God, Marcus, this is one of the reasons I love you so much," Dani exclaimed.

I put my arm around her waist, following behind my brother and Harper as we all made our way to the café.

"You love me because I bought you chocolate?" I asked jokingly.

"No. I love you because even when we aren't together, you're thinking of me. It's the little things you do that make me love you so much."

"But buying your wife a box of sweets while you're already in the store isn't very romantic," I drawled.

"I don't agree," she answered fiercely. "It's *very* romantic."

"If you say so," I replied skeptically.

She opened the bag and squealed happily. "Okay. This chocolatier is fantastic," she said enthusiastically. "This is amazing melted and warm. I love putting it on ice cream, but I have a better plan for it tonight."

I let out a startled cough. "And what would your plan be?"

"I'll surprise you."

I already had visions of us naked and Dani licking chocolate off one particular part of my body that already adored her. "I can't wait. Are you *really* hungry?"

"I'm starving," she answered cheerfully.

I'm fucked!

"But I can eat fast," she added teasingly.

"Take your time." I didn't want her to have to choke her food down just because she had a horny husband.

"I'll make sure it's worth waiting for," she answered in a seductive tone that always made me crazy.

I knew she'd make it worth crawling through hell for, which made it that much more difficult to delay the gratification.

We stopped our banter as we arrived at the café behind my brother and Harper.

Dani did indeed eat fast, but so did Harper and Blake, which made me wonder if they had a similar arrangement to mine and Dani's.

I inhaled my own food so fast that I hardly tasted it. Hell, what guy *wouldn't* when he knew that he was going to spend his evening in a state of unimaginable pleasure?

At the end of the meal, I pulled Dani out of our booth, dumping the check on my brother as we made our escape, citing a previous engagement.

"With who?" Blake asked skeptically.

"None of your business," I grumbled.

Blake snorted, but he picked up the tab so Dani and I could escape. Someday, I'd pay him back by picking up lunches or dinners together, but my mind was set on one person only right at that moment.

When we were finally in my vehicle and driving away from Main Street, I heard Dani sigh as she said, "Take me home, Marcus."

Hell, I couldn't drive fast enough. Her words made me feel like I'd been sucker-punched in the gut.

My house had actually become *home* to both of us, a mixture of old and new, hers and mine, and a place where I wanted to be all the time just because Dani was there with me.

I thought about my brothers and my sister, Chloe, each one of us finding love—one right after the other. Since I was the oldest, it really should have been *me* to settle down first. But I wasn't complaining. It had taken a special woman to put up with my ornery ass, and Danica had been well worth the wait!

~The End~

Acknowledgments

As always, I wanted to say thank you to my amazing KA team and my street team, Jan's Gems, for all they do to promote my books.

Thanks a million times to my readers. The Billionaire's Obsession series is on Book 11, and keeps getting more fun to write with every new couple. Thank you for loving my quirky, powerful, and sometimes very alpha billionaires.

I adore you all for letting me continue to do what I love so much as a day job!!

Xxx Jan

Please visit me at:
http://www.authorjsscott.com
http://www.facebook.com/authorjsscott

You can write to me at
jsscott_author@hotmail.com

You can also tweet
@AuthorJSScott

Please sign up for my Newsletter for updates,
new releases and exclusive excerpts.

Books by J. S. Scott:

The Billionaire's Obsession Series:

The Billionaire's Obsession

Heart of The Billionaire

The Billionaire's Salvation

The Billionaire's Game

Billionaire Undone

Billionaire Unmasked

Billionaire Untamed

Billionaire Unbound

Billionaire Undaunted

Billionaire Unknown

Billionaire Unveiled

Billionaire Unloved

The Sinclairs:
The Billionaire's Christmas
No Ordinary Billionaire
The Forbidden Billionaire
The Billionaire's Touch
The Billionaire's Voice
The Billionaire Takes All
The Billionaire's Secrets

The Walker Brothers:
Release!
Player!

A Dark Horse Novel:
Bound
Hacked

The Vampire Coalition Series:
The Vampire Coalition: The Complete Collection
Ethan's Mate
Rory's Mate
Nathan's Mate
Liam's Mate
Daric's Mate

Printed in Poland
by Amazon Fulfillment
Poland Sp. z o.o., Wrocław